THE GRACE OF
MARY TRAVERSE

TIMBERLAKE
WERTENBAKER

faber and faber

LONDON · BOSTON

in association with
the Royal Court Theatre

First published in 1985
by Faber and Faber Limited
3 Queen Square London WC1N 3AU

Phototypeset by Wilmaset Birkenhead Wirral
Printed in Great Britain by
Whitstable Litho Ltd Whitstable Kent
All rights reserved

All rights in this play are strictly reserved and
applications for performances should be made in
advance, before rehearsals begin, to Michael Imison
Playwrights Limited, 28 Almeida Street, London N1

British Library Cataloguing in Publication Data

Wertenbaker, Timberlake
The grace of Mary Traverse.
I. Title
812'.54   PS3573.E7/

ISBN 0-571-13886-1

For John

If you are squeamish

Don't prod the beach rubble

Sappho

Translated from the Greek by Mary Barnard
(University of California Press)

It may well be that it is a mere fatuity, an indecency to
debate of the definition of culture in the age of the
gas-oven, of the arctic camps, of napalm. The topic
may belong solely to the past history of hope. But we
should not take this contingency to be a natural fact of
life, a platitude. We must keep in focus its hideous
novelty or renovation . . . The numb prodigality of our
acquaintance with horror is a radical human defeat.

George Steiner, *In Bluebeard's Castle*
(Faber and Faber)

Master Carpenter	Chris Harding-Roberts
Deputy Master Carpenter	Tim Spencer
Stage Showman	Colin Neighbour*
Wardrobe Supervisor	Jennifer Cook
Wardrobe Assistant	Cathie Skilbeck
Trainee (Wardrobe)	Louise Stylli
	Susan Williams

YOUNG PEOPLE'S THEATRE

Director	Elyse Dodgson
Administrator	Carin Mistry
Youth Worker	Colin Watkeys

ADMINISTRATION

General Manager	Josephine Beddoe
Secretary	Susie Breakell
Membership Secretary	Vanessa Barker*
Literary Secretary	Jody Orgias*
Financial Administrator	Hilary Salmon
Financial Assistant	Terry Jones
Fundraiser	Ann Pennington*
Press and Publicity Officer	Sharon Keane
Press and Publicity Assistant	Natasha Harvey
House Manager	Toby Whale
Box Officer Manager	Christopher Pearcy
Box Office Assistants	Sally Harris
	Toby Spencer
Stage Door/Telephonist	Matthew Smith
Maintenance Supervisor	Tim Harrison
Cleaners	Eileen Chapman*
	Ivy Jones*
	Marie Toomey*
Evening Stage Door	Tyrone Lucas*
Head Usher	Valerie Gabbidon*
Head Barman	Hugh Merrell*
Firemen	Wilfrid Bartlett*
	Paul Kleinman*

* Part-time staff

The Royal Court Theatre
presents
the World Première of
The Grace of Mary Traverse
by
Timberlake Wertenbaker

Cast in alphabetical order

MR HARDLONG/JACK	David Beames
LORD GORDON/HANGMAN	Tom Chadbon
MRS TEMPTWELL	Pam Ferris
GILES TRAVERSE/	
LORD EXRAKE	Harold Innocent
MARY TRAVERSE	Janet McTeer
SOPHIE	Eve Matheson
BOY/GUARD/OLD WOMAN	Jonathan Phillips
MR MANNERS	James Smith

Other parts to be played by members of the company

Directed by	Danny Boyle
Designed by	Kandis Cook
Lighting designed by	Christopher Toulmin
Sound designed by	Andy Pink
Assistant Director	Michael Cooper
Stage Manager	Judi Wheway
Deputy Stage Manager	Audrey Cooke
Assistant Stage Manager	Barbara Bates
Production Photographs by	John Haynes
Poster design by	John Barraclough

First performance at the Royal Court Theatre on Thursday 17th
October 1985.

Although this play is set in the eighteenth century, it is not a historical play. All the characters are my own invention and whenever I have used historical events such as the Gordon Riots I have taken great freedom with reported fact. I found the eighteenth century a valid metaphor, and I was concerned to free the people of the play from contemporary preconceptions.

The game of piquet was devised with the help of David Parlett.

This is the script of the text as it was before rehearsals. Certain changes may have been made after this edition went to press.

Timberlake Wertenbaker

ACT ONE

SCENE ONE

The drawing room of a house in the City of London during the late eighteenth century. MARY TRAVERSE *sits elegantly, facing an empty chair. She talks to the chair with animation.* GILES TRAVERSE *stands behind and away from her.*

MARY TRAVERSE: Nature, my lord. (*Pause.*) It was here all the time and we've only just discovered it. What is nature? No, that's a direct question. Perhaps we will not exhaust nature as easily as we have other pleasures for it is difficult to imagine with what to replace it. And there's so much of it! No, that's too enthusiastic. (*Short pause.*) How admirable of you to have shown us the way, my lord, and to have made the grand tour of such a natural place as Wales. I believe there are mountains in Wales. Ah, crags, precipices, what awe they must strike in one's breas– in one's spirit. Yes. And I hear Wales has peasants as well. How you must have admired the austerity of their lives, human nature imitating the land's starkness. Peasants too, I believe, are a new discovery. How delightful is our civilization to shed such light on its dark and savage recesses. Oh dear, is that blue-stockinged or merely incomprehensible? But when you said the other day that when a man is tired of London he is tired of life, did you mean – but how foolish I am. It was Doctor Johnson. Forgive the confusion, you see there are so few men of wit about. (*Pause.*) You were telling me how we are to know nature. Do we dare look at it directly, or do we trust an artist's imitation of nature, the paintings of Mr Gainsborough. Whirlpools. Trees. Primordial matter. Circling. Indeed. Oh.

(MARY *stops in a panic.* GILES TRAVERSE *clears his throat.* MARY *talks faster.*)

You visited the salt mines? Ah, to hover over the depths in a basket and then to plunge deep down into the earth, into its very bowels.

GILES TRAVERSE: No, no, my dear. Do not mention bowels.

Especially after dinner.

MARY: To have no more than a fragile rope between oneself and utter destruction. How thrilling!

GILES: No, Mary. It shakes your frame with terror and you begin to faint.

MARY: I'd be too interested in what I was seeing to faint, Papa. I'd love to visit a salt mine.

GILES: You are here not to express your desires but to make conversation.

MARY: Can desires not be part of a conversation?

GILES: No. To be agreeable, a young woman must always make the other person say interesting things.

MARY: He hasn't said a word.

GILES: Ah, but he won't know that. Now faint, and even the most tongue-tied fop will ask how you are. That allows you to catch your breath and begin again.

MARY: And the rivers . . .

GILES: There's too much of this nature in your conversation.

MARY: It is what people are thinking about.

GILES: Sounds foreign. I shall bring it up at the next meeting of the Antigallican Society.

MARY: Oh, Papa, I know so much about it. Let me come and explain.

GILES: You? Now move on to another subject. This is difficult: leave no gap, you must glide into it. Converse, Mary, converse.

MARY: I can't think what follows naturally from nature. Ah, I hear God is . . . no . . . I believe God –

GILES: Talk of God leads to silence.

MARY: The architecture of –

GILES: Too athletic. People might think you spend time out of doors.

MARY: Reason, they say . . . is that too Popish?

GILES: No, but a woman talking about reason is like a merchant talking about the nobility. It smacks of ambition. I overheard that in a coffee house. Good, isn't it?

MARY: But, Papa, you're always talking about lords and you're a merchant.

GILES: I am not. Not exactly. Who told you this?

MARY: I look out of the window and see coaches with your name.

GILES: Why gape out of windows when I've given you so much to see in the house? I have land. There are potteries on it, but that's acceptable. Lord Folly has mines on his. It's vulgar to understand the source of one's wealth. Now if you have a Methodist preacher here and a rake there, how do you keep them from the weather and hunting?

MARY: Books? What does a rake read? Drink? That won't do.

GILES: It's obvious. Praise England: patriotism.

MARY: But, Papa, you won't let me study politics and I'd so like to.

GILES: Patriotism is to politics what the fart is to the digestion. Euh, you're not to repeat that, although it was said by a very grand lady. A Duchess. Say something against the Americans and fop, fool, rattle, mathematician and gambler will easily add to it.

MARY: Are we at war with them yet? Have you made another brilliant speech?

GILES: Yes. I proved conclusively that God gave us the colonies for the sole purpose of advantageous trade. We will talk to them about their raw material but never about their ideas. Upstarts! We'll finish now, I'm going to the theatre.

MARY: Let me come with you, Papa, it will help my conversation.

GILES: There's no need to see a play to talk about it. I'll bring you the play bill. We'll continue tomorrow with repartee, and do a little better I hope.

MARY: Wouldn't I do better if I saw a little more of the world, like you?

GILES: I'm afraid that's not possible. Don't be sad. You have tried today and I'll reward you with a kiss.

MARY: Thank you, Papa.

GILES: You are my brightest adornment, my dear. I want to be proud of my daughter.

MARY: Yes, Papa.

The drawing room. MARY, *alone, walks back and forth across a carpet. She stops occasionally to examine the area on which she has just stepped.*

MARY: Almost.

(She walks. Stops and examines.)

Yes. Better.

(She walks again. Looks.)

Ah. There.

(She walks faster now, then examines.)

I've done it: see the invisible passage of an amiable woman. *(Pause.)*

It was the dolls who gave me my first lessons. No well-made doll, silk-limbed, satin-clothed, leaves an imprint. As a child I lay still and believed their weightlessness mine. Awkward later to discover I grew, weighed. Best not to move very much. But nature was implacable. More flesh, more weight. Embarrassment all around. So the teachers came. Air, they said. Air? Air. I waited, a curious child, delighted by the prospect of knowledge. Air. You must become like air. Weightless. Still. Invisible. Learn to drop a fan and wait. When that is perfected, you may move, slightly, from the waist only. Later, dare to walk, but leave no trace. Now my presence will be as pleasing as my step, leaving no memory. I am complete: unruffled landscape. I may sometimes be a little bored, but my manners are excellent. And if I think too much, my feet at least no longer betray this.

(She walks.)

What comes after, what is even more graceful than air?

(She tries to tiptoe, then stamps the ground and throws her fan down.) Oh damn!

(She stands still and holds her breath.)

Mrs Temptwell!

(MRS TEMPTWELL *comes on immediately. Short silence.*)

4

My fan.

MRS TEMPTWELL: It's broken.

MARY: I dropped it.

MRS TEMPTWELL: A bad fall, Miss Mary.

MARY: Pick it up, please.

(MRS TEMPTWELL *does so*.)

MRS TEMPTWELL: I have work to do.

MARY: Fetch me some hot milk.

MRS TEMPTWELL: I'll call the chambermaid.

MARY: Wait. Watch me, Mrs Temptwell. Do I look ethereal?

MRS TEMPTWELL: You do look a little ill, Miss Mary, yes.

MARY: You don't understand anything. I'm trying not to breathe.

MRS TEMPTWELL: Oh yes. Your mother was good at that.

MARY: Was she? Tell me.

MRS TEMPTWELL: Said it thickened the waist. She died of not breathing in the end, poor thing, may she rest in peace, I'm sure she does, she always did.

MARY: Could she walk on a carpet and leave no imprint?

MRS TEMPTWELL: She went in and out of rooms with no one knowing she'd been there. She was so quiet, your mother, it took the master a week to notice she was dead. But she looked beautiful in her coffin and he couldn't stop looking at her. Death suits women. You'd look lovely in a coffin, Miss Mary.

MARY: I don't need a coffin to look lovely, Mrs Temptwell.

MRS TEMPTWELL: Some women don't even have to die, they look dead already, but that doesn't work as well. It's better to be dead and look as if you'd been alive than the other way, if you get my meaning, as if you'd been dead all the time, quiet and dull like.

MARY: I don't look like that.

MRS TEMPTWELL: Only when you've been reading.

MARY: I read all the time. (*Pause.*) Some books might make me feel a little dull. Caesar's Wars. The Young Ladies' Conduct. Travel books to places I'm not allowed to see.

MRS TEMPTWELL: It's a funny thing about books, they make the face turn grey. I had an uncle who took to books. He

5

went all grey. Then he went mad. May I go now?

MARY: When I tell you. Your uncle doesn't count. Books improve the mind.

MRS TEMPTWELL: That's as may be.

MARY: Have they not made me charming, witty?

(*Silence.*)

MRS TEMPTWELL: Now there's a girl down the street, in number fourteen. She's a lovely girl, Miss Mary, so lively. She's such a pretty sight, sitting at her window, staring at everything.

MARY: Gaping. How brutish. She has nothing to look at in her own house.

MRS TEMPTWELL: She even asked one of her servants to take her out on the street.

MARY: Outside? On foot? She did? Oh. But her reputation?

MRS TEMPTWELL: Disguised. No one will know. She said she wanted to know things, touch them, smell them. I wish you could see her, Miss Mary, she . . .

MARY: What?

MRS TEMPTWELL: Glitters with interest. Like a jewel.

MARY: Glitters? How vulgar. Fetch me my milk.

MRS TEMPTWELL: Your mother wanted to go out once in her life, but she died before we could manage it. I felt sorry she missed that one little pleasure in her quiet life.

MARY: Papa wouldn't have been pleased.

MRS TEMPTWELL: The master doesn't see everything.

MARY: Go away now.

MRS TEMPTWELL: The world out there isn't like the books.

MARY: What do you know about books, Mrs Temptwell?

MRS TEMPTWELL: I only know that the people out there are interesting and lively. The master doesn't read books.

MARY: No. What doesn't he want me to see?

MRS TEMPTWELL: I can't imagine. I'll fetch your milk now.

MARY: Wait. What's so different out there? When I ride in my carriage I see nothing of interest.

MRS TEMPTWELL: That's because the streets have to be emptied for your carriage. It's different on foot. Very different. Would you prefer a glass of ratafia?

6

MARY: Wait.

MRS TEMPTWELL: I haven't got all day.

MARY: What harm could once do? It'll only improve my
conversation and Papa will admire me. Yes. I'll be a
precious stone. Yes, Mrs Temptwell, you'll take me.

MRS TEMPTWELL: Take you where, Miss Mary?

MARY: You know what I mean. You'll take me out there. Yes.
In the streets.

MRS TEMPTWELL: I couldn't do that. I'd lose my place.

MARY: We'll go disguised. I've decided, Mrs Temptwell. You
suggested it.

MRS TEMPTWELL: I did not, Miss Mary. I never did.

MARY: Never mind, I'll pay you.

MRS TEMPTWELL: You always make me talk too much.

SCENE THREE

Cheapside, London. LORD GORDON *comes on.*

LORD GORDON: My name is George Gordon. Lord Gordon.
(*Pause.*) Nothing. No reaction. No one's interested.
(*Pause.*) It's always like this. I greet people, their eyes
glaze. I ride in Hyde Park, my horse falls asleep. (*Pause.*) I
am a man of stunning mediocrity. This can't go on. I must
do something. Now. But what? How does Mr Manners
make everyone turn around? Of course: politics. I'll make a
speech in the house. All criminals must be severely
punished. But stealing a handkerchief is already a hanging
matter. I know: make England thrifty and enclose the
common land. I think that's already been done. Starve the
poor to death! Perhaps politics is a little too ambitious. I'll
write. Even women do that now. But about what? No, I'll
be a wit. I'll make everyone laugh at what I say. But I'd
have to think of something funny. Sir John's a rake. That's
a possibility. But the ladies are so demanding and my
manhood won't always rise to the occasion. Shall I die in a
duel? No. Lord Luttrell's famous for winning a fortune at
gambling. How do I know I'll win? This is desperate. I

7

could at least dress outrageously. But that's so expensive. Perhaps I'm seen with the wrong people. They're all so brilliant. In a different world, I might shine. Here are some ordinary people. They must notice me, if only because I'm a lord. Oh, God, please make me be noticed, just once. Please show me the way.

(LORD GORDON *adopts an interesting pose. An* OLD WOMAN *comes on, walking slowly.*)

LORD GORDON: Hhm.

(*She looks at him and continues walking.* SOPHIE *comes on.*)

SOPHIE: Excuse me –

(*The* OLD WOMAN *turns around.*)

SOPHIE: No, you're not . . . I'm sorry. I'm looking for someone called Polly.

(*Pause.*)

My aunt . . . I'm to find her here. This is Cheapside?

(*The* OLD WOMAN *nods.*)

She has her pitch here. I've come to work for her. You don't know where she is?

(*The* OLD WOMAN *shakes her head.*)

I'm not sure what she looks like. I haven't seen her for a long time. (*Pause.*) Where could she be?

(*The* OLD WOMAN *shrugs.*)

SOPHIE: I don't know anyone.

(*The* OLD WOMAN *walks away.*)

What am I going to do?

(*The* OLD WOMAN *moves off.*)

London's so big.

LORD GORDON: Hhmm.

(SOPHIE *looks briefly at him and goes off.*)

SOPHIE: I must find Aunt Polly.

(MARY *and* MRS TEMPTWELL *come on.*)

MARY: I believe I've just stepped on something unpleasant, Mrs Temptwell. These streets are filthy.

MRS TEMPTWELL: The filth runs out of great houses like yours.

MARY: What? I don't like this world, it's nasty.

MRS TEMPTWELL: (*Sotto voce*) If you're squeamish, don't stir the beach rubble.

MARY: What did you say, Mrs Temptwell?

MRS TEMPTWELL: It's a saying we had in our family.

MARY: I always forget you had a family. I can't imagine you anywhere but in our house.

MRS TEMPTWELL: Lack of imagination has always been a convenience of the rich.

LORD GORDON: Hhmmm.

MARY: What? I do wish these people weren't so ugly.

(*The* OLD WOMAN *comes on.*)

MRS TEMPTWELL: Their life is hard.

MARY: They ought to go back to the country and be beautiful peasants.

MRS TEMPTWELL: They've come from the country. They've been thrown off the land. Some of them were farmers.

MARY: Papa says farmers stop progress. I meant beautiful peasants I could talk about with grace. There's nothing here to improve my conversation.

MRS TEMPTWELL: It takes time to turn misery into an object of fun.

LORD GORDON: (*Louder*) Hhhhmmmm.

MARY: Why does that man keep clearing his throat?

MRS TEMPTWELL: I don't know. He doesn't look mad.

MARY: I want to go back.

MRS TEMPTWELL: So soon? Such a dull appetite?

MARY: I might be curious about the plague and not care to embrace the dead bodies. This ugliness looks contagious.

MRS TEMPTWELL: Skin feels less soft when it's covered by coarse cloth.

MARY: I think you brought me out here to depress me with your dark mutterings. I'm going.

LORD GORDON: No. This is intolerable. You can't go without noticing me. My name is George Gordon. Lord Gordon. (*Silence.*)

MARY: Let's go.

LORD GORDON: How dare someone like you ignore me. You!

MARY: Mrs Temptwell, I'm frightened.

LORD GORDON: I don't want you to be frightened. Wait. Why not? Are you very frightened?

MARY: No, not very.

LORD GORDON: How dare you!

(*He takes out his sword.*)

Now. Now you're very frightened. I can see it. Why didn't I think of this before?

MARY: I want to go home.

LORD GORDON: Not yet. Not until you've been even more frightened. Yes. I'll show you my strength. Come over here to the lamppost.

MARY: Help!

(*The* OLD WOMAN *looks and walks as far from* LORD GORDON *as she can.*)

MARY: Mrs Temptwell!

MRS TEMPTWELL: This is the world.

(SOPHIE *comes on.*)

SOPHIE: Excuse me . . .

MRS TEMPTWELL: Damn!

SOPHIE: Oh. I'm sorry . . . Have you by any chance seen my aunt? Her name's Polly . . . What's there?

MRS TEMPTWELL: Nothing for you. Go away, girl. Quickly.

SOPHIE: But he –

MRS TEMPTWELL: So what? It could be you.

SOPHIE: Leave her alone, sir. What are you doing?

LORD GORDON: See how they come rushing towards me. Everyone pays me attention. Who are you? I'll have you too.

SOPHIE: Please, sir, please –

(LORD GORDON *grabs* SOPHIE. MARY *gets away.*)

LORD GORDON: Beg. Yes. Beg for mercy. Beg.

SOPHIE: Please have mercy, sir.

LORD GORDON: Ah. What a delight. Say over and over again, Lord Gordon have mercy on me. Say it.

SOPHIE: Lord Gordon have mercy on me. Lord Gordon have mercy on me.

LORD GORDON: Never has my name sounded so sweet. On your knees and keep saying my name.

SOPHIE: Lord Gordon.

LORD GORDON: My strength rises. I can't contain myself. Over here. Here.

MARY: We must call for help.

MRS TEMPTWELL: Why?

MARY: What will he do to her?

MRS TEMPTWELL: What he would have done to you. Rape her. But she won't mind. Virtue, like ancestors, is a luxury of the rich. Watch and you'll learn something.

MARY: Rape? What the Greek gods did? Will he turn himself into a swan, a bull, a shower of golden rain? Is he a god?

MRS TEMPTWELL: He'll feel like one.

MARY: He stands her against the lamppost, sword gleaming at her neck, she's quiet. Now the sword lifts up her skirts, no words between them, the sword is his voice and his will. He thrusts himself against her, sword in the air. He goes on and on. She has no expression on her face. He shudders. She's still. He turns away from her, tucks the sword away. I couldn't stop looking, but it's not at all as pretty as in the books and I think I'd rather be him than her.

(MR MANNERS *comes on.*)

MARY: Sir, be careful, there's someone –

MR MANNERS: Go away. I only give money to organized charities. Ah, Lord Gordon. I was looking for you.

LORD GORDON: Mr Manners. I was just thinking of you.

MR MANNERS: Have I disturbed you?

LORD GORDON: Not at all. I'm finished.

MR MANNERS: Who are these women?

LORD GORDON: Just women. What shall we do tonight, Mr Manners? I feel exceptionally lively.

MR MANNERS: We might play a game of piquet.

LORD GORDON: Yes. I'll win. My fortune has turned.

MR MANNERS: Delighted. Shall we have supper before?

LORD GORDON: I've never felt so hungry. Let's go to a chop house.

MR MANNERS: There's something on at the opera.

LORD GORDON: Yes, but first let's go to a coffee house. I have some witticisms.

MR MANNERS: You, Lord Gordon?

LORD GORDON: Mr Manners, I'm a different man.

MR MANNERS: What's happened? A legacy?

LORD GORDON: (*Quietly*) Power.

MR MANNERS: Ah. Power.

LORD GORDON: Isn't power something you know all about?

MR MANNERS: Yes, but it is not something I ever discuss.

(*They go off.* SOPHIE *comes down towards* MARY, *walking with pain. They look at each other. Then* SOPHIE *moves off.*)

MARY: Blood.

SCENE FOUR

Outside the Universal Coffee House in Fleet Street. BOY, *an eighteenth-century waiter, blocks* MARY *and* MRS TEMPTWELL.

BOY: You can't.

MARY: They've just gone in.

BOY: You can't come in.

MARY: We're following them.

BOY: Ladies wait outside.

MRS TEMPTWELL: Ask him why?

MARY: Why?

BOY: That's the way it is. (*Pause.*) They don't like to be disturbed.

MARY: I won't disturb them. I know how to talk.

BOY: They don't do ladies talk.

MARY: What sex is wit?

MRS TEMPTWELL: Ask him who's in there.

BOY: Mr Fielding, Mr Goldsmith, Mr Hume, Mr Boswell, Mr Garrick, the Doctor, Mr Pope, Mr Sheridan, Mr Hogarth.

MARY: But I know them all very well. I've read them. I've talked to them many times in my imagination. Let me in immediately.

BOY: And some foreigners. Mr Corelli, Mr Piranesi, Mr Tiepolo, Mr Gluck, Mr Hayden, Mr Voltaire, Mr Leibniz, Mr Wolfgang. They're quiet the foreigners and no one listens to them. You have to stay out. Orders.

MRS TEMPTWELL: Ask him why they let him in.

BOY: I'm the boy. I go everywhere.

12

MARY: I don't understand.

BOY: I'll let you see through the window.

MARY: I've spent my life looking through misted window panes. I want to face them.

BOY: Wouldn't be right.

MARY: I have the right to.

MRS TEMPTWELL: Doesn't right belong to those who take it?

BOY: I don't ask questions.

MRS TEMPTWELL: Wouldn't you like to be like him?

MARY: Yes. No. Envy is a sin, Mrs Temptwell. Yes, and heaven must be a lady's tea party: the jingling of beatific stupidity. What's happened to me? I was happy in my rooms, but out here I feel a cripple's anger. I can't touch or smell this world. Mrs Temptwell, you lied to me.

MRS TEMPTWELL: Think of what you've seen.

MARY: I've seen them walk the streets without fear, stuff food into their mouths with no concern for their waists. I've seen them tear into skin without hesitation and litter the streets with discarded actions. But I have no map to this world. I walk it as a foreigner and sense only danger.

BOY: I never stay anywhere long. I get bored. There's too much to do.

MARY: Be quiet!

BOY: I was only being pleasant because I feel sorry for you.

MARY: Pity's violence with the gloves on. Go away!

BOY: It's a waste of time being kind to women. They're not grateful.

MARY: I'm going to hate you! No, that's an ugly feeling. But it's there. I hate you.

MRS TEMPTWELL: Why waste your time hating him, Mary? You could be like him if you wanted to. But there's a price. You might not want to pay it.

BOY: Her soul.

MRS TEMPTWELL: We're not so medieval, boy. We're Protestants and the century's enlightened. Do you want to walk the world the way they do? Do you want to travel in their world?

MARY: It looks very interesting . . .

MRS TEMPTWELL: No rebuffs. No doors ever closed. Around every corner the glitter of a possibility. Do you want that?

MARY: I think so . . .

MRS TEMPTWELL: You'll no longer be an ornate platter served for their tasting. No, you'll feast with them, nothing forbidden, no taste untried.

MARY: Yes.

MRS TEMPTWELL: No part of flesh or mind unexplored. No mystery unnamed. No horizon ever fixed.

MARY: Experience!

MRS TEMPTWELL: Yes. Is that what you wish for?

MARY: Yes. Never to have to hold my breath in again, nor my thoughts. Oh yes.

MRS TEMPTWELL: I could manage it for you.

BOY: We're not deceived when they dress as men. A lady came to us masqueraded. We uncovered her. All of her.

MRS TEMPTWELL: Do I sound so superficial? Well, Mary?

MARY: Will I be allowed to run the world through my fingers as they do? Yes? I want it. Yes. I want it all. What's the price?

MRS TEMPTWELL: You'll come with me.

MARY: Of course. But the price?

MRS TEMPTWELL: You can never go back.

MARY: Will I want to?

MRS TEMPTWELL: They've never asked to live like us.

MARY: No, they're too busy. I'll be too busy. I won't want to go back. But I want the world as it is, Mrs Temptwell. No imitations. No illusions.

MRS TEMPTWELL: You'll know all you want to know.

MARY: Shall we sign a contract?

BOY: Here are your witnesses.

(LORD GORDON *and* MR MANNERS *appear*.)

MRS TEMPTWELL: It's already done. You can go back inside, boy.

BOY: It's more interesting out here this evening.

MR MANNERS: What is happening here, boy?

BOY: I don't know. I don't understand it.

MRS TEMPTWELL: See now, Mary, who's outside.

MARY: Yes, yes. How will I pay you, Mrs Temptwell?

MRS TEMPTWELL: Don't worry. You'll pay.

14

ACT TWO

SCENE ONE

The Brothers Club. GILES TRAVERSE, MR MANNERS.

MR MANNERS: Three days?

GILES: Three.

MR MANNERS: And the letter?

GILES: Only that her dear Papa would understand, she'd gone
to investigate the very underside of nature. I thought she
meant Vauxhall Gardens. I don't approve, of course, but
Lord Oldland told me his daughter often went to Vauxhall,
masked, and never came to any harm. Mary is such a
sensible girl.

MR MANNERS: Have you told anyone?

GILES: No. I went to Bow Street.

MR MANNERS: My dear Giles, you might as well have gone
straight to the papers.

GILES: It is my daughter, Mr Manners. She could have been
kidnapped, she could be hurt.

MR MANNERS: This isn't France. You said she left with a
servant. An elopement?

GILES: No. Mr Manners, you must know someone who can
investigate, discreetly.

MR MANNERS: No one in politics can afford the cost of a secret,
not even you, Giles. No. There's nothing you can do.
Forget her.

GILES: Forget my daughter!

MR MANNERS: Do you think Lord Oldland knows where his
children are, or who they are, for that matter?

GILES: I have only one daughter.

MR MANNERS: You have only one country. The King, Giles,
wants new men in the Cabinet. Men of intelligence and
ambition, men who show strength of character. There has
been mention of you. But should there be a scandal . . .

GILES: The Cabinet? Now?

MR MANNERS: I had the impression you had a strong sense of
duty. Perhaps I was wrong . . . These are difficult

times . . . Times of change.

GILES: After all these years. Why now?

MR MANNERS: You of all people should know: supply and demand. People have become suspicious of the old families. But the old families do know how to conduct themselves . . .

(LORD GORDON *comes on.*)

LORD GORDON: Giles. Just the man I was looking for.

GILES: My lord.

LORD GORDON: I have made a momentous decision. Yes. I've decided to get married. It's what I need: a wife to look up to me. I want to marry your daughter.

GILES: You've seen her!

LORD GORDON: How could I? You've never presented her. I don't want to marry a woman I know. You've said your daughter's pretty and clever. She's not too clever, is she? She won't talk at breakfast? I couldn't bear that. But she's very young, isn't she, and she won't be used to speaking to a lord . . .

MR MANNERS: You're too late, Gordon. Giles' daughter died yesterday, of a bad chill.

GILES: Mr Manners!

MR MANNERS: I know how painful it is for you, Giles. We won't mention her again.

LORD GORDON: How inconvenient. I'll have to think of something else. You don't have any other daughters, do you?

GILES: No. No one but Mary. Mr Manners –

MR MANNERS: At least she went quietly, Giles, we must be thankful for that. I'll speak to the King, he may find a way to ease your grief. Kings have such curative powers . . .

SCENE TWO

The study of GILES TRAVERSE. *He is in some disarray.* MRS TEMPTWELL *is dressed for the street.*

GILES: Where is she?

16

MRS TEMPTWELL: Don't you know? You buried her.

GILES: Who are you?

MRS TEMPTWELL: I've been in this house thirty years, sir.

GILES: I know that, Mrs Temptwell. Why have you done this?

MRS TEMPTWELL: Done what, sir? Been a good servant? I've always done what Mary asked. She used to want cups of tea. Now she wants other things.

GILES: I'll have you thrown in prison.

MRS TEMPTWELL: For what? Killing her? I might have to tell people she's still alive. Think of the questions . . .

GILES: I trusted you with the care of my daughter. Was Mary not kind to you?

MRS TEMPTWELL: As she might be to the chair she sat on. Yes, she cared for my use.

GILES: What more can a servant expect?

MRS TEMPTWELL: When I was a child, I read as much as Mary.

GILES: People ought not to be educated beyond their position in life. Did I let Mary read too much?

MRS TEMPTWELL: Do you remember my father?

GILES: I remember most of my servants.

MRS TEMPTWELL: He was a farmer when you were a farmer. His land was next to yours.

GILES: I must have bought it.

MRS TEMPTWELL: He trusted you to leave him his cottage. But when you landscaped your garden, you needed a lake. The cottage was drowned in the lake.

GILES: I gave those people work.

MRS TEMPTWELL: He went to one of your potteries. He died.

GILES: And it's because of your father's misfortune that you've killed my daughter?

MRS TEMPTWELL: Your daughter's only dead for you. That's your misfortune.

GILES: Please tell me where she is.

MRS TEMPTWELL: She's not ready to see you. She hasn't yet learned to be a ghost.

GILES: I'll give you anything you want.

MRS TEMPTWELL: You've already done that.

GILES: I don't understand. I don't understand at all.

MRS TEMPTWELL: It's simple, Giles Traverse. When a
man cries, he could be anybody.

SCENE THREE

Lodgings in Marylebone. MRS TEMPTWELL *stands in the*
background and watches. MARY *is fully dressed.* MR HARDLONG *is*
naked. They are far apart.

MR HARDLONG: You ask for pleasure. Why do you cringe as if
expecting violence?
(*Short silence.*)
If you believe violence will bring you pleasure, you've been
misled. The enjoyment of perversion is not a physical act but
a metaphysical one. You want pleasure: come and take it.
(*Silence.* MARY *does not move.*)
Are you pretending you've never felt desire unfurl in your
blood? Never known the gnawing of flesh, that gaping
hunger of the body? Never sensed the warm dribble of your
longings? Come, come, need isn't dainty and it's no good
calling cowardice virginity.
(MARY *squirms a little.*)
Perhaps you want me to seduce you and let you remain
irresponsible? I promised you physical pleasure, not the
tickle of self-reproach and repentance, the squirm of the
soul touching itself in its intimate parts. Or are you waiting
for a declaration of love? Let romance blunt the sting of
your needs, mask a selfish act with selfless acquiescence.
Novels, my dear, novels. And in the end, your body
remains dry. What are you waiting for? Pleasure requires
activity. Come.
(MARY *moves a little closer and closes her eyes.*)
Ah, yes. Close the eyes, let the act remain dark. Cling to
your ignorance, the mind's last chastity. A man's body is
beautiful, Mary, and ought to be known. I'll even give you
some advice, for free: never take a man you don't find
beautiful. If you have to close your eyes when he comes
near you, turn away, walk out of the room and never look

18

back. You may like his words, his promises, his wit, his soul, but wrapping your legs around a man's talent will bring no fulfilment. No, open your eyes and look. Look at me.

(MARY *looks, unfocused.*)

The neck is beautiful, Mary, but doesn't require endless study. Look down. The arms have their appeal and the hands hold promise. The chest can be charming, the ribs melancholic. Look down still. They call these the loins, artists draw their vulnerability, but you're not painting a martyrdom. Look now.

(MARY *focuses.*)

See how delicate the skin, how sweetly it blushes at your look. It will start at your touch, obey your least guidance. Its one purpose to serve you and you'd make it an object of fear? Look, Mary, shaped for your delight, intricacies for your play, here is the wand of your pleasure, nature's generous magic. This is no time for hypocritical restraint. I'm here for you. Act now. You have hands, use them. Take what you want, Mary. Take it.

(MARY *stretches out her hand.*)

MARY: At first, power. I am the flesh's alchemist. Texture hardens at my touch, subterranean rivers follow my fingers. I pull back the topsoil, skim the nakedness of matter. All grows in my hand.

Now to my needs. Ouch! No one warned me about the pain, not so pleasant that. Scratch the buttocks in retaliation, convenient handles and at my mercy. And now to the new world. Ah, but this is much better than climbing mountains in Wales. I plunge to the peaks again and again with the slightest adjustment. One, two, three, change of angle, change of feel. Ah, this is delightful and I'm hardly breathless. Again. Not Welsh this, the Alps at least: exploding sunshine, waterfalls, why is this geography not in the books? On to the rolling waves of the Bay of Biscay, I would go on for ever, why have you stopped, Mr Hardlong, have you crashed on the Cape?

You don't answer, Mr Hardlong, you're pale and short of breath. I am the owner of this mine and there are seams still untouched. You mustn't withdraw your labour. You seem a little dead, Mr Hardlong. I need your work and must revive you. I want more, much more.

MRS TEMPTWELL: We'll have to find you someone else, Mary.

MARY: I like this one. I love you, Mr Hardlong, yes, I do. I thought I loved my father, but that was cold. This is hot. Don't turn away, Mr Hardlong, oh please don't die.

MRS TEMPTWELL: Don't be sentimental. Labour's expendable.

MARY: He's reviving. Oh joy. Mr Hardlong!

MR HARDLONG: Where's my gold?

MARY: Here, Mr Hardlong. Take it. Bring food to revive us, Mrs Temptwell. A duck, some good roast beef, and a pudding of bread and butter, very sweet. You'll eat with me, Mr Hardlong.

MR HARDLONG: I don't have time. Where is she?

MARY: Who?

MR HARDLONG: You promised she'd be here, Mrs Temptwell.

MRS TEMPTWELL: I haven't forgotten. (*She calls*) Sophie!
(SOPHIE *comes on, bringing food*. MARY *pounces on it*.)

MARY: (*Eating*) I've seen you before. I remember now. Lord Gordon. I was sorry.

MRS TEMPTWELL: (*Touching* SOPHIE's *stomach*) Observe how mediocrity loves to duplicate itself. There's the rest of your payment, Mr Hardlong.

MR HARDLONG: (*To* SOPHIE) Come with me.

SOPHIE: Mrs Temptwell, you didn't tell me –

MRS TEMPTWELL: Do you want to starve on the streets?

MR HARDLONG: Don't be afraid, I won't hurt you.

SOPHIE: You said I was to work for a lady.

MRS TEMPTWELL: So you are. Mr Hardlong's price was high. You're saving Mary half her gold. That's what servants are for.

MR HARDLONG: Come quickly.

MARY: Mr Hardlong?

MR HARDLONG: Look. I have gold.

MARY: Mr Hardlong!

MR HARDLONG: What is it? You see I'm in a hurry.

MARY: Please answer one question. I paid you a good sum for

what we did.

MR HARDLONG: Fifty guineas.

MARY: You'll give it to Sophie.

MR HARDLONG: All of it.

MARY: For the same thing we did?

MR HARDLONG: The same.

MARY: I'm young. My flesh is new. I pay you. You pay her. I don't understand.

MR HARDLONG: I gave you pleasure, Mary.

MARY: Yes. You did.

MR HARDLONG: Did you offer me any?

MARY: I confess I forgot a little about you. But weren't we doing the same thing?

MR HARDLONG: I looked after your well-being.

MARY: I see, yes. We were at the same table but I let you go begging while I was feasting. And Sophie?

MR HARDLONG: Will serve my luxury.

MARY: I would do that too, Mr Hardlong. I would advocate the community of pleasure. Teach me what to do.

MR HARDLONG: It's too late, Mary: you would have to learn to ask for nothing.

(MR HARDLONG *and* SOPHIE *go.* MARY *begins to eat pensively, but none the less grossly.*)

MARY: Which do I like best? The first taste of sauce on palate, or the crinkled feel of roast skin on the tongue. And when the bones crack, the pleasure is in power. Metaphysical? I like to swallow too. I'm still hungry.

(*She eats.*)

It's not really hunger, is it, Mrs Temptwell? It's a void in the pit of my stomach. Knowledge scoops out its own walls and melancholy threatens. What comes next, Mrs Temptwell, what comes next? I didn't have to leave my rooms to learn that nature abhors a void. Give me more, quickly, give me something more.

A large den in Drury Lane. LORD EXRAKE *and* MR MANNERS *are playing piquet.* MARY, SOPHIE *and* MRS TEMPTWELL *come on.*

MR MANNERS: *Carte blanche.*

(LORD EXRAKE *discards five cards.*)

MARY: Cards. Numbers, chance, mystery and gain. Oh, what a rich and generous world.

MRS TEMPTWELL: For some.

MARY: Don't be glum, Mrs Temptwell. Let me enjoy it all.

LORD EXRAKE: *Seizième.*

MARY: And look over there, a cock fight. Man transmutes nature's savagery into gold for himself, the once elusive magic stone is nothing but greed. Shall we go there or play cards? What do you want to do, Sophie?

SOPHIE: Me? . . . I don't know . . .

MRS TEMPTWELL: Our Sophie has no desires.

SOPHIE: Please . . .

MARY: But causes desires in others and so maintains the world's harmony. I don't understand the world yet, but I will, I will.

MR MANNERS: You're over the hundred, Lord Exrake.

LORD EXRAKE: Am I, dear boy? So I am, so I am.

MARY: You play cards, Sophie, I'll go and watch the fight.

SOPHIE: I can't.

MARY: I'll give you the money and you can keep what you win.

SOPHIE: No.

MARY: Try a little pleasure, Sophie, do.

MRS TEMPTWELL: Those used to hunger don't make gluttons, isn't that so, Sophie?

SOPHIE: What? I don't understand . . .

MARY: Another damp northern saying. Ignore her. Let's play cards.

MRS TEMPTWELL: They may not let you.

MARY: What will you wager on that?

MRS TEMPTWELL: Be careful.

MARY: Why?

MR MANNERS: Piqued, repiqued and capoted. You have all the luck tonight, Lord Exrake.

LORD EXRAKE: At my age, dear boy, there is no luck, only science. (*He sees the women.*) Ah, look, beauties are approaching us. We are having a visitation from the fair sex. Let us hail them . . . You owe me four hundred and fifty pounds, Mr Manners.

MR MANNERS: Won't you play another game, Lord Exrake and let me win back some of my losses?

LORD EXRAKE: No, no, dear boy, don't win, don't win. *Qui perd au jeu gagne à l'amour* and, of course, vice versa. Do they still teach you young boys French? Ah, *l'amour, l'amour.* What good is gold without *l'amour.* Is that not so, mesdemoiselles?

MARY: No, my lord, for what love does not eventually have to be paid for? I'll play with you.

LORD EXRAKE: Will you, my dear? There is not so much here as there once was. Come and sit on my lap.

MARY: I meant piquet, my lord. I'll sit opposite your lap.

MR MANNERS: He's not playing any more.

LORD EXRAKE: Oh, but I didn't say . . . Mr Manners, one does not refuse a lady . . .

MR MANNERS: The gambling is serious here.

MARY: Is money ever frivolous, Mr Manners?

MR MANNERS: The stakes are high, you do not want to play.

MARY: I can pay.

LORD EXRAKE: Indeed, mademoiselle, a beautiful young lady can always pay, one way or another, we shall come to an amicable arrangement.

MARY: I do not need to sell my flesh, my lord, and yours might not fetch enough. Shall we play for money? You may choose the stakes.

LORD EXRAKE: You are blunt, mademoiselle, you remind me . . . Ten shillings a point?

MRS TEMPTWELL: That's too high, Mary.

MARY: Shall we double it?

MR MANNERS: A pound a point. Don't play, Lord Exrake.

23

MARY: Are you his keeper?

MR MANNERS: I believe in keeping a sense of decency in these proceedings.

MARY: Is risk indecent, Mr Manners? Shall we make it two pounds a point, Lord Exrake?

LORD EXRAKE: Two pounds . . . What is your name?

MARY: Mary.

MR MANNERS: Your other name?

MARY: Do you mean my patronymic? I have none. I'm unfathered.

LORD EXRAKE: (*To* SOPHIE) And you, my pretty? Forgive me for not noticing you before, mademoiselle. You're not as tall as your friend but not so fierce neither. I think I like you better.

MARY: Her name's Sophie. Let's play.

LORD EXRAKE: Sophie . . . such a beautiful name . . . You remind me . . .

(MARY *cuts the cards.*)

MARY: I am elder.

LORD EXRAKE: And I the youth. Ah, youth. It was as a mere youth . . . have I told you, Mr Manners?

MR MANNERS: Yes, you have.

MARY: Point of five.

LORD EXRAKE: Making?

MARY: Forty-nine.

LORD EXRAKE: Good.

MARY: In hearts. Lord Exrake, it is my hand that should interest you, not my legs. Keep your feet to yourself.

LORD EXRAKE: Alas, you'd hobble me, mademoiselle. It was thinking of my youth . . . mademoiselle Sophie . . . can you not make allowances? Where is the beautiful Sophie? Come and sit on my lap, your friend is too severe. That is, if your dear mama will allow.

MARY: She's not our mama, she's our duenna, keeps the grim suitor, prudence, from our hearts.

MRS TEMPTWELL: Do what you want with her, Lord Exrake, she never resists.

SOPHIE: Mrs Temptwell, please –

MR MANNERS: You ought not to be here, Mary, I know who you are.

MARY: How can you, when I do not even know myself? Do you know yourself, Mr Manners?

MRS TEMPTWELL: Concentrate on the game, Mary.

MARY: And a cart major.

LORD EXRAKE: Good. Do sit on my lap, belle Sophie, your friend frightens me.

MARY: You stand behind me, Mr Manners. Shall I invite you on my lap?

MR MANNERS: I want to watch you play.

MARY: Ah: a voyeur. And I took you for a man of action. That's five for point, four for the sequence nine.

LORD EXRAKE: No, no, do not try to escape, dear Sophie.

MRS TEMPTWELL: She has nowhere to escape.

MARY: Three knaves?

LORD EXRAKE: Three knaves are not good.

MARY: I feel your suspicions down my neck, Mr Manners, I know you do not trust the fairness of the fair sex. Defend my reputation, duenna, tell him I've encountered fortune head on, no female coyness for me. And one's ten.

LORD EXRAKE: I count fourteen tens and three queens. You talk too much. It is not that I mind women who talk, in the salons, women used to speak, but in the salons, they spoke in French . . . Do you know the salons, Mr Manners?

MR MANNERS: No. Your discards are good, Mary.

MARY: Yes. One learns. To discard. Yours too must be good, Mr Manners.

MR MANNERS: It is more natural in a man.

MARY: Perhaps nature is no more than practice. Eleven, twelve, thirteen, fourteen, fifteen.

LORD EXRAKE: Seventeen. The salons . . . Mlle de Lespinasse. Would you like an introduction, although now . . . she spoke to me in the strictest confidence . . . I was much in demand . . . Nineteen, twenty, twenty-one, twenty-two, twenty-three.

MARY: Seventeen, eighteen and ten for cards, twenty-eight. I've won.

MR MANNERS: Well played, your hand was weak.

MARY: Did you take me for a fool?

MR MANNERS: I don't make quick judgements.

MARY: Then you lack imagination. Second deal.

MR MANNERS: Imagination is one of my best discards.

MARY: You are the elder, Lord Exrake.

LORD EXRAKE: Alas, I am, I am. Now. Once . . . *l'Anglais*
gallant, they called me. Some wag said an *Anglais* gallant was a
contradiction in terms, but Mlle de Lespinasse . . . *Les
Anglais*, she said, ah *les Anglais*. Such phlegmatic exteriors,
but beneath *tout cela*. *Quel* fire, she said, what *feu*. It does
indeed make the saying true that an Englishman's home is his
château and what a château. *Les Anglais* . . .

(LORD EXRAKE *has discarded hesitantly and picked up his
cards*.)

Point of seven.

MARY: Good.

LORD EXRAKE: I have met Italians, she said, no more than
gesture deep. Cart minor.

MARY: Not good.

LORD EXRAKE: And the Spanish, who like scorpions, sting
themselves to death with their own passion. A trio of kings.

MARY: Not good.

LORD EXRAKE: Ah. Mm. And the Dutch. The Dutch . . . One
for the heart makes eight.

MARY: (*Triumphantly*.) *Seizième* for sixteen, a *quatorze* of
knaves, a trio of aces, that's thirty-three and the repique
ninety-three.

LORD EXRAKE: She had travelled. Would you like to travel with
me, Sophie? Your friend plays too well.

(*They play out their tricks*.)

MARY: That is yours.

LORD EXRAKE: It was on my travels I met mademoiselle
Sophie, or was it Sylvie? . . . She was with that writer. But
he wrote so much and pleasure needs time. It is a
demanding vocation, like war. *A l'amour comme à la
guerre*. The rest are yours, I believe.

MARY: No, a soldier braves death but obeys authority. The

26

pleasure seeker braves authority but obeys annihilation.
This makes pleasure the heroism of the disobedient, the
rebel's pastime. War is for those who dare not step out of
line. This makes a soldier a coward, an interesting paradox
is it not, Mr Manners? Four for five.

MR MANNERS: I don't like paradoxes, they give me bad dreams.

LORD EXRAKE: I have ten for cards and final score twenty-four.

MARY: And I have exactly one hundred.

MRS TEMPTWELL: That's one hundred and seventy-six or three
hundred and fifty-two pounds. Stop now, Mary.

MARY: Another game, Lord Exrake?

LORD EXRAKE: I too was bold when I was young. I believed I
had time to waste.

(*They play.*)

MARY: I don't waste time, I love it, I am time's lover.

LORD EXRAKE: But it isn't wasted time that's so painful, no,
wasted time is time that never existed. It's the memories.

MARY: Memories are for the idle. I'll never be idle.

LORD EXRAKE: Memories . . . those leeches of the mind,
exquisite moments that now suck you dry.

MARY: I shall never have memories.

MR MANNERS: Everyone has memories, but it is possible to
change a people's memory.

MRS TEMPTWELL: My memories are my reason for being.

SOPHIE: I like mine.

MARY: I'll know so much there will be no time for memories.

LORD EXRAKE: I suffer the torment of Tantalus. If I could
reach out my hand I'd live those moments again. Do you
understand me?

MARY: No. I score one hundred and twenty.

LORD EXRAKE: Sixty. It isn't the fear of death that keeps me
here all night.

MARY: I sleep as little as I can, the world gives me so much
pleasure.

LORD EXRAKE: Keeps me here all night, pawing at youth, it's
the fear of those memories. The moments mock me with
their vanished existence. You'll see.

MARY: I'm afraid of nothing, Lord Exrake, least of all of your

27

warnings. I've won again. That's another two hundred and thirty-four pounds. I've lost count of the total.

MRS TEMPTWELL: Two thousand six hundred and eighty-eight pounds. That's what Lord Exrake owes you.

MARY: Another game?

LORD EXRAKE: No, no. You remind me of my youth.

MARY: And you have failed to remind me of my old age. Look, look. All this money. I do love to win. Come, Sophie, what shall we do now? There's more to win somewhere. Two thousand pounds. I could double it before dawn.

(LORD GORDON *comes on.*)

LORD EXRAKE: It was the first time I slept through the dawn that the memories took over. There were suddenly too many years between me and the new day. Do I make myself clear? They buzz in my ears and I can't hear.

(MARY *turns away, to* LORD GORDON.)

MARY: How's your cock, Lord Gordon?

LORD GORDON: Bruised from the last encounter. Do I know you?

MARY: Mine's fighting fit. Will you pit it against mine?

LORD GORDON: I never bet against a woman. Your face . . .

MARY: Afraid of bad luck? Scratch a parliamentarian, you find a follower of folk tales.

SOPHIE: Mrs Temptwell, it was him.

MRS TEMPTWELL: So?

LORD GORDON: (*To* MARY) When my cock recovers, perhaps.

MARY: Cocks recover so slowly and I presume you have no spare?

(MR HARDLONG *comes on. The men ignore him.*)

LORD GORDON: I have seen you before.

MR MANNERS: Someone you wanted to marry?

LORD GORDON: I couldn't marry a woman with such an active voice. There's something . . .

MARY: How can I remember someone who won't expose his cock? Are you looking for me, Mr Hardlong?

MR HARDLONG: No, for Sophie.

MARY: Who will fight my cock?

LORD EXRAKE: I have one.

28

MARY: So, so. Wondrous nature. Is it ready?

LORD EXRAKE: Spurred and trimmed. I've left your friend. She's charming but too quiet. At my age one needs a challenge, so I've come back to you.

MARY: I too need a challenge, Lord Exrake, and I'd prefer to dare Mr Hardlong's cock. Will you, Mr Hardlong?

MR HARDLONG: If Sophie will stand by me.

MRS TEMPTWELL: She'll do what we tell her.

MR MANNERS: You ought to choose more carefully who you bet with, Mary.

MARY: I didn't escape from propriety to fall into snobbery.

MR MANNERS: That's a mistake. Snobbery is cheap to practise and has saved many a nonentity.

MARY: Just so. I don't need it. Where's my whip, Mrs Temptwell?

MRS TEMPTWELL: Here. Don't bet too much.

MARY: Two hundred and fifty guineas, Mr Hardlong?
(*They touch their whips.*)

LORD EXRAKE: I remember . . . although ladies didn't have cocks in those days.

MARY: Nature is so changeable it can only be female. Now, my bird, fight for me, match my courage and my strength.
(*The birds fight. Screams and urgings from all.*)

MR MANNERS: Your cock's dead.

MARY: Why do you want to depress me, Mr Manners?

MR MANNERS: I'm only telling you what is.

MARY: No, look. Look. It was a ruse. My cock's risen and stricken Mr Hardlong's. Ha! You see, Mr Manners, it is not so easy to say what is. Your facts may be ruses too.

MR HARDLONG: My cock's failed me.

MARY: That happens, Mr Hardlong, even to the best. And I triumph again. I keep winning. I keep winning. What now? What is there to do? What can I spend money on?

MR HARDLONG: Will you come and console me, Sophie?

MARY: Mr Hardlong, it is I who have the money. Will you come to me? No, you're an exhausted experience, no longer virginal. Sophie, come here. Closer. Here. Two hundred and fifty guineas.

29

SOPHIE: Oh, no, I can't.

MRS TEMPTWELL: Take it.

SOPHIE: Thank you, Miss Mary.

MARY: Yes, but you must work for it.

(*Pause.*)

Nothing for nothing. That's their law. When they offer you money, you know what for. What are you waiting for?

SOPHIE: I don't understand.

(MARY *lifts up her skirts to* SOPHIE.)

MARY: Men don't know their way around there. You will.

SOPHIE: I –

MARY: Look. Surely it's more appealing than their drooping displays? Or do you share their prejudice? What is it, gentlemen, you turn away, you feel disgust? Why don't you look and see what it's like? When you talk of sulphurous pits, deadly darkness, it's your imagination you see. Look. It's solid, rich, gently shaped, fully coloured. The blood flows there on the way to the heart. It answers tenderness with tenderness, there is no bottomless pit here, only soft bumps, corners, and cool convexities. The voracious darkness is no more than the gaping void of your own minds. This is generous and full of gratitude. Ah, Sophie, how sweet you are, I understand why they love you, but I can love you more than they ever have. Such peace. I feel sad. Shall we sleep? No – look, over there, the spectres of passing time. I can't bear it. What can we do?

(TWO OLD WOMEN *have limped on.*)

LORD GORDON: (*To* MR MANNERS) Did you hear what happened last night at Brook's?

MR MANNERS: No, the Americans kept us all night in the Cabinet. It's a most trying country.

LORD GORDON: Lord Darling and Mr Worth raced two woodlice. Lord Darling's won. He's being talked about all over town. Lucky man.

MR MANNERS: Shall we go there? I'm bored.

MARY: That's a way to make money in an amusing manner. If animals and insects will work for us, why not them? Mr Manners, shall we race the old ladies? You cannot question my choice of opponent.

MR MANNERS: Why not?

MARY: Three thousand pounds?

MRS TEMPTWELL: That's all the money we have.

MR MANNERS: Set them up, Hardlong.

(*The* TWO OLD WOMEN *are walking side by side.* LORD
GORDON *raises his arm and everyone begins to urge them on.
They start to run as fast as they can, which is very slowly,
coughing, panting and stumbling.*)

MR MANNERS: Faster, faster. There's a good girl.

MR HARDLONG: Odds on Mr Manners's hag. Go. go.

LORD GORDON: Mr Manners's hag has just taken the lead. Miss
Traverse's hag having a little trouble.

MARY: I'll whip you if you stumble again. Pick your feet up.

MR MANNERS: Come on, you can do it.

LORD GORDON: Miss Traverse's hag catching up. Is she? Yes,
she is. No, she's tripped.

MARY: Your hag tripped mine, Mr Manners, I saw it.

LORD GORDON: No, there was no foul play. Mr Manners's hag
still in the lead.

MARY: Get up quickly, go on, go on.

LORD GORDON: Miss Traverse's hag a little winded. Making an
effort, yes, she's closing the gap. Can she do it?

MARY: You can do it.

MRS TEMPTWELL: Three thousand pounds. We'll go hungry if
she loses.

LORD GORDON: Mr Manners's hag is slowing down. Miss
Traverse's hag getting ahead. What a race.

SOPHIE: We've been well fed.

MRS TEMPTWELL: Crumbs off her plate.

MARY: Faster. Faster.

SOPHIE: She's ahead. She'll win. Faster. Faster.

MRS TEMPTWELL: You're cheering yourself on. That could be
us.

SOPHIE: You cheer her on.

MR HARDLONG: Let me take you away.

LORD GORDON: Miss Traverse's hag well in the lead. Mr
Manners's hag stumbles.

31

MR MANNERS: Steady, girl, steady.

LORD GORDON: Only a few steps to the finishing line. It looks like Miss Traverse's hag. But no. Look. Oh, what a jump, look at that, what an effort and is it? Yes. It is. It's Mr Manners's hag first. What a superb effort. What a close race. But it's Mr Manners's hag.
(*Shouts.*)

MARY: He cheated. Mr Hardlong gave her brandy.

MR MANNERS: It's not against the rules.

LORD GORDON: Mr Manners never breaks rules. You owe him three thousand pounds.

MRS TEMPTWELL: Don't give it to him. He likes you. Cry. Faint. Offer him –

MARY: What, Mrs Temptwell. You'd have me look female now? You disappoint me.

MRS TEMPTWELL: (*To* SOPHIE) We go hungry to save her appearances.

MARY: Three thousand pounds, Mr Manners. You've made me lose.

MR MANNERS: I have that effect on many people. Where's my hag? Here's a shilling for you. You ran well.
(*The other* OLD WOMAN *approaches* MARY, *who ignores her.*)

OLD WOMAN: Please, miss.

MARY: Let's go.

OLD WOMAN: I ran for you.

MARY: And you lost. Go away, don't touch me.

OLD WOMAN: I've been ill. Have pity.

MARY: Ask nature to have pity on you.

OLD WOMAN: Be kind.

MARY: Why? Look around. Do you see kindness anywhere? Where is it? Where?

OLD WOMAN: Give me something.

MARY: I'll give you something priceless. Have you heard of knowledge?
(*She takes the whip and beats her.*)
There is no kindness. The world is a dry place.

OLD WOMAN: Please.

MARY: What, you want more?

(*She beats her. The* OLD WOMAN *falls.*)

MRS TEMPTWELL: (*To* SOPHIE) Isn't that your Aunt Polly?

MARY: Have I hurt her?

(*She bends down and looks at her.*)

I've seen her before. Or was it her sister? Yes. I have seen
her before. Why do you all stare at me? She was standing
outside church. My father told me to give her some money.
He gave me a coin. I gave her the coin, smiling. She smiled.
I smiled more kindly. My father smiled. I followed his
glance and saw a lady and a young man, her son, watching
me. They were smiling. My father gave me another coin. I
moved closer to her, my steps lit by everyone's smiles. I
remember watching the movement of my wrist as I put the
coin in her hand. I smiled at its grace. (*Pause.*) Was that
better? Tell me, was that better?

(*Fade.*)

INTERVAL

ACT THREE

SCENE ONE

Vauxhall Gardens at night. MARY *and* MRS TEMPTWELL *stand in the dark, waiting. Music and lights in the background.* MARY *has a rounded stomach under dirty clothes.*

MRS TEMPTWELL: Voices. Coming this way.
> (*They listen.*)

MARY: They've turned down another path.

MRS TEMPTWELL: They're coming closer.

MARY: I tell you they've turned away. Your hearing's blunt.
> (*They listen.*)

MRS TEMPTWELL: Footsteps on the grass.

MARY: Yes. (*She listens.*) They're not his.

MRS TEMPTWELL: You can't know that. Shht.

MARY: Those footsteps bounded my happiness for eighteen years, I'd recognize them now. I feared and loved them. Now I fear nothing and love nothing either. Damn. This itch.
> (*She scratches herself. Listens.*)
> Shht. No.

MRS TEMPTWELL: Are you miserable?

MARY: You're waiting for my yes, aren't you? You'll chew on that yes like a hungry dog, spit it up and chew again. Well, you can beg for your yes. Do a trick for me, Mrs Temptwell, entertain me. Say something interesting. You know I hate silence. And stop smiling.

MRS TEMPTWELL: I wasn't smiling, you're seeing things.

MARY: I saw your evil grin through the darkness. Cover up your teeth, please, they make me ill.

MRS TEMPTWELL: It's your condition, I told you to sit.

MARY: Damn this leech in my stomach, sucking at my blood to wriggle itself into life. Why can't you do something about it, you old wizard?

MRS TEMPTWELL: If I was the devil we wouldn't have to shiver in Vauxhall Gardens waiting for our supper.

MARY: I could kill the man who did this. I found him in the

34

Haymarket, he looked strong, seemed to have some wit and the night was soft and thick. We went to Westminster Bridge, I liked that, the water rushing beneath me, cool air through my legs, until I discovered he was wearing a pigskin. New invention from Holland, he explained. He wouldn't catch my itching boils and I'd be protected from this. Fair exchange. So I had this piece of bookbinding scratching inside me and his words scratching at my intelligence. I'd mistaken talkativeness for wit. I hope he caught my infection. Footsteps. No. Why is it the one time I had no pleasure my body decided to give life? What's the meaning of that? Why don't you answer? Why do you never say anything? Has it ever happened to you? Were you ever young? Answer my questions, damn you. Who are you?

MRS TEMPTWELL: It won't interest you.

MARY: You don't know what interests me.

MRS TEMPTWELL: If you had an interest in anybody else you wouldn't have thrown all your money away.

MARY: I was trying to determine whether greed was the dominant worm in the human heart. The experiments were costly. You didn't have to stay.

MRS TEMPTWELL: I hear something.

MARY: Let's rob the first person who comes.

MRS TEMPTWELL: Don't you want to see him? Find out how deeply he's mourning his dead daughter?

MARY: How easily he cancelled my existence. (*Pause.*) Tell me a story.

MRS TEMPTWELL: I don't know any.

MARY: Go away then. You were well fed in my father's house. Why don't you go back? Do you enjoy this misery?

MRS TEMPTWELL: Times will get better.

MARY: Time gets faster or slower but never better. I won't mind if you go.

MRS TEMPTWELL: I'll stay.

MARY: Then distract me, damn you. Tell me your story. Where were you born? Don't you dare not answer.

MRS TEMPTWELL: The country.

MARY: The country. The country. There are trees here.

MRS TEMPTWELL: The North.

MARY: I know that from your granite face. Where?

MRS TEMPTWELL: Don't shout or they'll hear us.

MARY: Then talk. Remember something.

MRS TEMPTWELL: I had a grandmother.

MARY: I had a grandfather.

MRS TEMPTWELL: She was hanged as a witch.

MARY: That's better.

MRS TEMPTWELL: That's all.

MARY: Aren't there laws now against hanging witches?

MRS TEMPTWELL: It depends on the magistrate.

MARY: And she taught you to cast spells?

MRS TEMPTWELL: She was an old woman, and poor. She talked
    to herself because she was angry and no one listened.

MARY: Tell me more. Tell me everything.

MRS TEMPTWELL: They put a nail through her tongue.

MARY: How was she dressed? Stop hoarding your words, you
    old miser.

MRS TEMPTWELL: She was naked. I remember how thin she
    was. And the hair, the hair between her legs. It was white.
    That's all I remember.

MARY: Did people cry?

MRS TEMPTWELL: They laughed. I laughed too once I'd
    forgotten she was my grandmother. The magistrate laughed
    loudest. She'd been on his land and he'd taken her cottage
    but she stayed at his gates. She asked for justice, he heard a
    witch's spell.

MARY: How interesting to have so much power and still so
    much fear.

MRS TEMPTWELL: He enjoyed her humiliation. Everyone did.

MARY: That's something I've never experienced.

MRS TEMPTWELL: Nothing stops you. It's easy.

MARY: Why when I hear a tale of cruelty do I want to do the
    same? Are we imitators by nature or is every crime already
    dormant in the heart waiting only to be tickled out?

MRS TEMPTWELL: Footsteps. On the gravel.

MARY: His.

MRS TEMPTWELL: Cover your face.

36

MARY: What about yours?

MRS TEMPTWELL: He's never looked at me.

(GILES *and* SOPHIE *appear. She is leading him.*)

GILES: Where are you taking me, my sweet? No need to come this far.

SOPHIE: I'm afraid of being seen, sir.

GILES: Let's stop at this tree.

SOPHIE: This way, sir.

GILES: I'm in such a hurry.

MARY: Here, sir.

GILES: Who's that?

MRS TEMPTWELL: A woman, sir, they're all the same.

GILES: Sophie, where are you?

MRS TEMPTWELL: Forget Sophie, she's docile but dull. Look here.

GILES: I can't see anything.

MARY: Here, sir, I'll entertain you.

MRS TEMPTWELL: She's fanciful and clever and I'm practical and knowing, if not so young.

GILES: I want a woman, not a personality. Sophie . . .

MRS TEMPTWELL: She is our drawbridge, the treasures are inside.

MARY: Here, sir.

MRS TEMPTWELL: Go to Mary.

GILES: Mary . . .

MRS TEMPTWELL: Lovely name, Mary, isn't it?

GILES: Sophie's young. I want someone very young.

MARY: I'm young, sir, and know things Sophie doesn't know. Don't turn away, sir, rejection is so painful. Come here.

GILES: If it means that much to you . . . This isn't a trick? You're not more expensive?

MRS TEMPTWELL: Labour is cheap, there's too much of it. And it's lazy, not as good as the machines. Perhaps one day this too will be done by machines. Would you like that?

GILES: At least machines don't talk.

MARY: I'm told my conversation is my greatest charm, sir. Come here.

GILES: It's so dark.

MARY: Who wants light, sir? Isn't light the greatest mistake of our
century? We light the streets and stare at dirt. As for the
lantern we poke into nature's crevasses, what has it revealed?
Beauty or the most terrifying chaos? If I take a close look at
nature now, I mean your nature, what will I find?
(*As she talks, she unbuttons* GILES.)
That it's tame, sir, most tame, but our gardeners have
taught us to make it wild, with the help of a little art.

GILES: (*Feebly*) Must you talk quite so much?

MARY: It's my father who taught me to talk, sir. He didn't
suspect he'd also be teaching me to think. He was not a
sensitive man and didn't know how words crawl into the
mind and bore holes that will never again be filled. What is
a question, sir, but a thought that itches? Some are mild,
the merest rash, but some are prurient, contagious, without
cure. Do you have children, sir, to grace your old age? Men
often tell me I remind them of their daughters. You look
sad, sir, is your daughter dead? Did she die of a chill? That
happens with women of graceful breeding, the blood
becomes too polite to flow through the body. Or fever? She
hid tropical desires under a cold skin? As long as she died
young, men prefer that. Age, after all, is a manly quality.
But even manly age, it seems, needs a little help if we're to
get anywhere. A rub, will that do?
(*She begins to massage him.*)
It helps men to think of their daughters when I do this.
You didn't kill yours, did you? Ah, I see it works. We're
ready. Front or back? Oh, the bird's already flown the
cage. Happens. Must have been the thrill of my
conversation. Or thinking of your daughter.
(MARY *uncovers her face.*)
But you recognized your daughter some time ago, Papa, by
the grace of her conversation.
(*Pause.*)
How did you say your daughter died? Did you starve her
with your puny rations of approval? But she's here. Look.

GILES: I have no daughter.

MARY: My name is Mary Traverse. Your wife had little chance

38

of fathering me elsewhere. I am your daughter.

GILES: You're a whore.

MARY: Is a daughter not a daughter when she's a whore? Or can she not be your daughter? Which words are at war here: whore, daughter, my? I am a daughter but not yours, I am your whore but not your daughter. You dismiss the my with such ease you make fatherhood a deed of possession, torn at will. Or is it your act of grace? An honour I can only buy with my graces? These discarded, I fall from your grace and free you of fatherhood because I disgrace you.

GILES: What do you want from me?

MARY: Two things. Look at me.

GILES: Tell me what you want.

MARY: I'm here, Papa. Here. Look at me!
(*Pause.* GILES *looks.*)
Good.

GILES: Why? I gave you everything.

MARY: Except experience.

GILES: You could have married a lord.

MARY: I said experience, not a pose. The world outside, all of it. This.

GILES: This! I did everything to keep you from this! I didn't live in a beautiful house like you as a child. I had to work hard. Very hard. I was able. I made money, started the potteries, bought land, made more money. Everything I make sells now. I wanted you to have the ease, the delights I never knew. I wanted to protect you from what I had experienced, protect you even from the knowledge I had experienced it.

MARY: You took my future to rewrite your past. Oh father, don't you see that's worse than Saturn eating his own children?

GILES: I let you read too much, you've gone mad.

MARY: And when I try to explain, you threaten me with a madhouse? How dare you!

GILES: I forbid you to talk to me in that manner!

MARY: You have no power over me, Papa. Your daughter's dead. Now for the second thing. I want money.

39

GILES: Here's twenty guineas.

MARY: Money, Papa. Not its frayed edges.

GILES: It's the agreed price for a whore.

MARY: If I wanted to make money lying on my back, I would have married your lord. I am not a whore, Papa.

GILES: But – you –

MARY: I learn. I do not whore.

GILES: I don't understand. Why – but if – you – if you're not – we can forget. I'll find a way to bring you back. Explain. It wouldn't matter. If you would come back . . . as you were . . .

MARY: As your graceful daughter?

GILES: My daughter, my beautiful and witty daughter.

MARY: Open your eyes. Look at me again.

(GILES *looks. Silence.*)

Do you want me back?

(*Silence.*)

The father I want cannot be the father of 'your' daughter. And yet I'm not so hardened I don't want a father. Could you try to be 'my' father?

GILES: I'll send you a little money.

MARY: I see. I want half of your money.

GILES: No.

MARY: A small price to keep me dead, Papa. Your powerful friends are supping in these gardens. Shall I walk through the tables and cry you've whored your daughter? I'll be believed. I talk well. People love to think ill. Don't try to cheat me. I know how much you have. The factories, the machines, the shops, the land, the canal.

GILES: What's made you like this?

MARY: Experience is expensive and precise.

GILES: I can tell you one thing, Mary. At the end of all this, you'll find nothing. Nothing. I know. Goodbye.

(*He leaves.*)

MARY: The only time he says my name, it's to curse me. One more denial. And he can still make the world grow cold.

MRS TEMPTWELL: Did you see the humiliation on his face? I loved it.

MARY: Why?

MRS TEMPTWELL: The magistrate who hanged my
    grandmother was his brother.

MARY: So?

MRS TEMPTWELL: You wouldn't understand.

MARY: I no longer understand anything. Suddenly.

MRS TEMPTWELL: At least you experienced cruelty. Their
    cruelty.

MARY: Is that what it is?

MRS TEMPTWELL: Didn't it give you pleasure?

MARY: No. Sadness. And then, nothing. Nothing. The
    withering of the night. I'm cold.

SCENE TWO

Vauxhall Gardens. SOPHIE *by herself. Then* JACK.

JACK: By yourself?

SOPHIE: Yes.

JACK: Always by yourself?

SOPHIE: Yes!

JACK: Want company?

SOPHIE: Yes.

JACK: No one to look after you.

SOPHIE: No.

JACK: Not here for the toffs!

SOPHIE: No!

JACK: I hate them.

SOPHIE: Yes?

JACK: Fat. We go hungry.

SOPHIE: Yes.

JACK: Hungry?

SOPHIE: Yes.

JACK: Here. Good?
    (JACK *hands her some bread.*)

SOPHIE: Yes.

JACK: Stole it.

SOPHIE: Yes?

JACK: Dangerous. But not wrong.

SOPHIE: No.

JACK: Ever seen them work?

SOPHIE: No.

JACK: Come here.

SOPHIE: Yes.

JACK: Jack.

SOPHIE: Jack. Yes. Jack.

> (*They kiss.*)

SCENE THREE

Vauxhall Gardens. MR MANNERS, LORD GORDON.

MR MANNERS: The mob can be good or the mob can be bad, Lord Gordon, it depends on whether they do what you want them to do.

LORD GORDON: I could lead them. I could lead anything if I were made into a leader. It's getting there I find difficult.

MR MANNERS: Real power prefers to remain invisible.

LORD GORDON: I wouldn't mind not having the power. Just make me visible. Notorious.

MR MANNERS: What can I do? I'm a servant.

LORD GORDON: You, Mr Manners? The man most feared in Parliament?

MR MANNERS: A mere servant, I assure you. The power I serve is awesome.

LORD GORDON: The King?

MR MANNERS: The King's only a human being, Gordon, a German one at that. No, I serve a divine power.

LORD GORDON: You don't mean God, you haven't become a Methodist?

MR MANNERS: Order, Gordon, order. The very manifestation of God in the universe. Have you studied the planets?

LORD GORDON: Can't say I have, no. I look at 'em.

MR MANNERS: Ordered movement, everything in its place, for ever. That's why I like men who make machines. They understand eternal principles, as I do. As you must.

LORD GORDON: I'm good at adding.

MR MANNERS: When you ride in your carriage, you mustn't sit back and loll in your comfort, no, you must study the smooth functioning of the vehicle, and if a wheel falls off, take it as a personal affront. Do you understand?

LORD GORDON: Check the wheels of my carriage . . .

MR MANNERS: So with the country. We must watch that no wheel falls off.

LORD GORDON: Do we wear splendid livery?

MR MANNERS: What?

LORD GORDON: I would like to serve the country.

MR MANNERS: Good.

LORD GORDON: When can I start?

MR MANNERS: We must wait. The times are restless.

LORD GORDON: (*Triumphant*) The roads are bumpy!

MR MANNERS: And dangerous.

LORD GORDON: Highwaymen lurking behind every tree!

MR MANNERS: I think we've exhausted that, Gordon. It is clear we must find something new, entertaining.

LORD GORDON: Me!

MR MANNERS: Who knows? Someone's . . . inevitably there. Or something . . .

LORD GORDON: Be good to have me. Keep them quiet.

MR MANNERS: Who?

LORD GORDON: The families, you know, my uncle. The other old families.

MR MANNERS: What do they say?

LORD GORDON: That they wouldn't invite you to their house. Have to invite me. I'm a relative.

MR MANNERS: What else do they say?

LORD GORDON: Nothing much. Used to rule England, time to rule again, better at it, born to it, look at the mess, all that. I don't listen.

MR MANNERS: In times such as these different people appear, make different claims. The good servant looks for what fits best into the order of things. It is not always obvious.

LORD GORDON: I'm here, Manners, as soon as you want a change.

MR MANNERS: No, no, Lord Gordon, you haven't understood. Whatever happens, nothing must change.

SCENE FOUR

Lodgings. MARY *and* SOPHIE. *Silence.*

MARY: I'm cold.

SOPHIE: Are you ill, Miss Mary?

MARY: No. Bored with a boredom that chills the marrow of my bones. In which part of the anatomy does sadness sit, do you know, Sophie? And if the body's a machine why is the human soul so chaotic? My father's right. I'm too clever. The inside of my skin hurts.

SOPHIE: Here's Mrs Temptwell with your milk.

(MRS TEMPTWELL *comes on.*)

MARY: Take it from her and tell her to go.

MRS TEMPTWELL: Mary –

MARY: Make her go, Sophie.

MRS TEMPTWELL: Mary –

SOPHIE: Mary wants you to go, Mrs Temptwell. Go away.

(MRS TEMPTWELL *leaves. Silence.*)

MARY: How's your child?

SOPHIE: He died.

MARY: Did he? I didn't know. (*Pause.*) I'm sorry. (*Pause.*) Am I? Are you?

(*Silence.*)

MARY: You can have mine.

SOPHIE: Oh yes, Miss Mary, I'd like that, please.

MARY: Why?

SOPHIE: Why what?

MARY: No. I don't want to know why. What's that noise?

SOPHIE: Shouting. The price of white bread has gone up again.

MARY: I thought you people ate brown bread.

SOPHIE: We don't like it. Our teeth aren't strong enough to eat brown bread. The merchants are hiding their sacks of flour to make prices go up so the people have decided to find the sacks and take them by force. Then they'll sell them at a

44

fair price. Jack says it's happening all over the country. People are very angry. They've beaten some merchants.

MARY: Would you do that if you were hungry?

SOPHIE: Oh no.

MARY: If you were very hungry? I would. But I don't have to. Do you ever think about that?

SOPHIE: About what?

MARY: Come here. Closer. We're the same age. Why do you never look at me? (*Pause.*) Look into my eyes.

SOPHIE: They're very beautiful, Miss Mary.

MARY: What do you think of me?

SOPHIE: You're feverish, Miss Mary, I'll get you more milk.

MARY: I asked you a question. What do you think of me?

SOPHIE: I don't understand.

MARY: You have a mind. It must function occasionally. Tell me what it sees.

SOPHIE: The country, Miss Mary. Fields. The fields I used to walk in as a child. That's what it sees. Green.

MARY: What questions does it ask?

SOPHIE: Questions?

MARY: A question is a sentence that begins with a how, what, why and ends in a whimper.

SOPHIE: Yes. How I can be less tired. Why my belly hurts. Is that what you call thinking? And what a good thing white bread is. Sometimes I think about the baby, but not much.

MARY: What do you think about me?

SOPHIE: I think about getting your milk quickly and how not to spill it.

MARY: About my life.

SOPHIE: I hope it will be a long one.

MARY: Are you pretending to be stupid?

SOPHIE: I don't understand, Miss Mary.

(*Pause.*)

I feel things.

MARY: What do you feel for me? Hatred? Contempt? Don't be afraid. Answer.

SOPHIE: I don't feel – that way. I feel the cold. And the heat even more than the cold.

45

MARY: Sophie!

SOPHIE: I don't have time to think the way you do. Please, Miss Mary, let me get you some hot milk.

MARY: No. Do I disgust you?

SOPHIE: You found me on the streets. I had nothing.

MARY: But I pushed you on the streets as well. You took my place with Lord Gordon. What did you feel then? What did you feel in the gambling den, servicing my pleasures? What did you feel?

SOPHIE: I don't know. I can't remember. Sometimes I don't feel I'm there. It could be someone else. And I'm walking in the fields. So I don't mind much. My brother used to touch me. He was strong and I learned to make it not me. I was somewhere else. But when I want to, with Jack, I'm there. And then not. It's not difficult.

MARY: I see. I'm not sorry then. Perhaps I never was. It seemed natural for you to take my place. I only thought about it because I'm bored. But I'm even more bored. Send me Mrs Temptwell, tell her to come with some ideas.

(MRS TEMPTWELL *comes on*.)

MRS TEMPTWELL: I'm here, Mary. I knew our quiet Sophie wouldn't entertain you for long. You can go, Sophie.

MARY: No, let her stay.

(*Silence*.)

Well?

MRS TEMPTWELL: I've seen some beautiful jewels we could acquire.

MARY: Jewels.

MRS TEMPTWELL: There are women wrestling in Clerkenwell, you like that.

MARY: Do I?

MRS TEMPTWELL: Do you want to go abroad?

MARY: What for?

(*Pause*.)

Well?

MRS TEMPTWELL: You could gamble if you promise not to lose everything.

MARY: I've already done that. What else?

46

(Silence.)

MARY: This is intolerable. Will I have to kill myself to make the time pass? Something. Something. And I can't sleep. Do you have dreams, Sophie?

SOPHIE: I dream of a little cottage . . .

MARY: Oh, stop.

SOPHIE: Jack dreams of a new world.

MARY: A new world? Does he? A new world . . . Who's Jack?

SOPHIE: He's . . . Jack. He's very handsome.

MARY: They're all handsome when we drape them with our longings. A new world . . . Even Sophie's Jack has more interesting thoughts than I do, Mrs Temptwell. Why?

MRS TEMPTWELL: You're tired.

MARY: No. Action. I want action. But what? What?

MRS TEMPTWELL: I've told you.

MARY: What? Another endless round of puny private vice? This isn't experience, Mrs Temptwell, this is another bounded room. You promised more, remember? No horizon ever fixed? No mystery unnamed? This is nothing. What do they do when they're bored? Ah. I know. They make wars, slash at the blinding dullness, cover up the silence with screams, I understand that now.

MRS TEMPTWELL: We could go to America.

MARY: Or they dream of new worlds. They let their imagination roam freely over the future, that's what they do. They think about their country and then they rule the country. Why didn't you tell me? What sort of a new world does Jack dream of, Sophie?

SOPHIE: Nobody has too much. Kindness. Villages, everybody the same. I don't remember it all. It's free.

MARY: Free. But that's beautiful. Why doesn't he shout it from the rooftops?

SOPHIE: He's not good at talking.

MARY: I am. I'll talk for him. A new world. Such a simple and lovely phrase, it rests on hope, kindness, yes, no smallness, no meanness, no pinched stomachs and minds. A world not ruled by my father or Mr Manners with their large greed and petty ambition, a world ruled by us for our

47

delight. Free. Bring me to Jack, Sophie, let's start the new world.

MRS TEMPTWELL: You're raving.

MARY: If you wish to talk like my father you can stay at home.

MRS TEMPTWELL: I never said you could be exactly like them.

MARY: I won't. I'll know their power, but I'll use it for the good.

SCENE FIVE

In front of the Houses of Parliament. The GUARD *stops* MARY *and* JACK. TWO OLD WOMEN *come on during the interchange, then a* LOCKSMITH, *then* GILES.

GUARD: I told you: no petticoats in the Houses of Parliament.

MARY: I'll unpetticoat myself if it's my underwear you object to. What I have to say is without frills.

JACK: Listen to her.

GUARD: I know you, you're the one who keeps bringing petitions.

MARY: No petticoats, no petitions, what do you allow in that house which is supposed to represent us all?

GUARD: What?

MARY: We'll change history if we go in there. Don't you want a change?

GUARD: No.

MARY: You're young. Wouldn't you like a different world?

GUARD: No.

MARY: Imagine a world where no one was born to suffer and no one born to make others suffer. No masters in there, no slaves out here.

GUARD: Who're you calling a slave?

MARY: Wouldn't you like a world where everyone was free to choose their future?

GUARD: Not much.

MARY: Oh, the precious maidenhead of a young man. No virgin shuts her legs as tight as you your mind. No new thought

48

will ever penetrate to make you bleed.

GUARD: Watch your language, Miss.

MARY: Why are you guarding a power that excludes you, that has no interest in your well-being? Don't you see this authority you worship is feeding off your body, your mind, your life? Listen to me, don't turn your face to the wall. What are they doing for you in there? What?

JACK: Yes. What?

GUARD: And what would your world do for me, eh?

MARY: It would do what you wanted it to do because you would be making it. The world will no longer be ruled by the rich and powerful who abuse us, restrict us, enslave us and kill us. Ask yourself who gave them that right? What have they done to deserve such power? Nothing. Their family stole it a long time ago and then kept it. This will stop. Our sons and daughters will share the land.

OLD WOMAN: I'm not giving anything to my daughter. She's a whore.

MARY: In the new world, there will be no whores, there won't have to be.

LOCKSMITH: If I want a whore and I can pay for her I have a right to that whore. It's nobody's business.

MARY: No. No one will have their pleasure at the cost of another's pain. Everyone will have their equal, natural, just share of pleasure.

LOCKSMITH: I'm not having a woman tell me what my rights are.

MARY: Why not, if it's common sense?

JACK: We want justice, equality, everyone can speak.

MARY: There will be no greed, no hoarding of riches, no more theft.

LOCKSMITH: What happens to the locksmiths?

MARY: It is wrong, it is unnatural, it is unreasonable –

LOCKSMITH: I'm a locksmith. What good are locks without thieves?

MARY: – for a few families who do nothing to keep all the wealth and make us wretched. You will make keys for all of us.

49

LOCKSMITH: Oh. No. You get paid more for locks than keys.

JACK: Freedom for all of us.

MARY: Do you know how much our king costs us? Eight hundred thousand sterling a year. How much bread does that buy?

OLD WOMAN: I saw the King the other day. He looks ever such a gentleman.

LOCKSMITH: Why don't you go to America if you don't like it here? They make you pick cotton in the heat there and you die in two weeks.

MARY: Who was the first king of England? A French bandit. And it's the descendants of his band of robbers who are bleeding us now. What does the King do for us? He makes us fight wars we don't care about. Has he ever asked us what we wanted, what we needed?

LOCKSMITH: If that was my daughter I'd have her locked up.

GILES: Why? She speaks well. What she says is wrong, of course.

MARY: We must work together and imagine together this new world. We must share in its building and its delights.

JACK: We want the brotherhood of man.

MARY: The new world will be just, gentle, wise, free, uncircumscribed.

GILES: I used to think like that.

MARY: We will have a society free of the unnatural yoke of government. No more walled fortresses where they laugh at us and never let us in. Ask yourselves why we have no bread to eat?

OLD WOMAN: I've asked that before. No one tells me.

MARY: Ask yourselves why our children are born to hunger and toil.

OLD WOMAN/GUARD: Why?

(MR MANNERS *comes on from the Houses of Parliament*.)

MARY: Ask yourselves why they never ask us what we need.

ALL: Why?

MR MANNERS: Why do you say all this out here and not in there?

MARY/ALL: Yes. Why?

MR MANNERS: They'd like to have you in there. They're most
interested in what you have to say.

JACK: We're not allowed in there.

MR MANNERS: That can change.

MARY: You'll let us into the House?

MR MANNERS: Not the House exactly, but there are many
rooms. I have some friends who wish to talk to you.

MARY: Let's go.

MR MANNERS: Just you – for the moment.

JACK: Go in, Mary, talk to them.

MARY: I'll see what they have to say and come back.

(MARY *and* MR MANNERS *leave*.)

GUARD: She was better out here.

GILES: People were listening. She made people listen.

JACK: She'll talk to them and come back.

GUARD: I've seen people go in there and come out very
different.

JACK: We have to make everyone listen. Even them.

GUARD: Are you going to this new world?

LOCKSMITH: I'm not having a world without locks.

SCENE SIX

Preparations for a midnight conversation. MRS TEMPTWELL *and*
SOPHIE *set out chairs.*

MRS TEMPTWELL: We must stop her.

SOPHIE: Why? She's so gay.

MRS TEMPTWELL: And us? What happens to us?

SOPHIE: She said I could go to the country and look after her
child.

MRS TEMPTWELL: No.

SOPHIE: Please don't stop me from having the child.

MRS TEMPTWELL: She had you raped, she made you whore,
she caused the misery that killed your child and now you
want to slave to bring up her reject. Why?

SOPHIE: She said we could have a cottage.

51

MRS TEMPTWELL: Until she takes it away to make way for some roses. Don't you know what she's like, her and the rest of them?

SOPHIE: Who?

MRS TEMPTWELL: The masters, girl, all of them. Listen to these words, Sophie, listen: freeborn Englishman. Aren't they sweet?

SOPHIE: I suppose so.

MRS TEMPTWELL: My father was a freeborn Englishman. So was yours.

SOPHIE: I never knew him.

MRS TEMPTWELL: But us? I'm a servant. Nothing my own, no small piece of ground, no hour, no sleep she won't break with a bell. Nothing. Do you understand, girl?

SOPHIE: I don't know. Did you suffer misfortune?

MRS TEMPTWELL: He was our misfortune, her father. My father had to work for him who wasn't any better than us, no. We watched our mother grow thin as hunger and die. I curse the family, her, and all the likes of her.

SOPHIE: You could get another place.

MRS TEMPTWELL: She'll be as low as us when I'm finished. And you'll help, Sophie.

SOPHIE: I don't feel low.

MRS TEMPTWELL: When you know all I know you'll be angry too.

SOPHIE: When I've been angry, it's only made it all worse. No. I won't be angry. Is that all the chairs?

MRS TEMPTWELL: We'll work together. I'll be a friend.

SOPHIE: You said that when you brought me to the house.

MRS TEMPTWELL: I didn't know she was so vicious. Now she'll do even more harm with these ideas of hers.

SOPHIE: I like it when she speaks of the new world. So does Jack.

MRS TEMPTWELL: New world? This is no way to get rid of the old.

A midnight conversation: the last stages of a drunken dinner.
SOPHIE, MRS TEMPTWELL, MARY, JACK, *the* GUARD, LORD
GORDON, MR MANNERS.
MARY: Sophie, wine for the gentlemen and for me.
MR MANNERS: No more for me.
MARY: Moderation in all things, Mr Manners?
MR MANNERS: Historical moments need level heads.
MARY: Why? The future is intoxicating.
JACK: I'm a working man. I drink gin.
MRS TEMPTWELL: And gin for me.
MARY: I forgot you, Mrs Temptwell.
MRS TEMPTWELL: That's what happens to working people,
    Jack, when they're no longer useful.
GUARD: It's all going to change now.
MRS TEMPTWELL: Is it?
MARY: Mrs Temptwell used to dream as much as we do, Jack,
    but one day she turned back and like Lot's wife became a
    pillar of bitter salt.
LORD GORDON: That's a woman's lot. Ha, ha, ha.
    (*Silence.*)
MARY: We are here to work out our common cause and to find
    its simplest expression.
LORD GORDON: Do you like gin, Jack?
JACK: More than anything.
SOPHIE: But you like me best of all, don't you, Jack?
JACK: That's a sweet lass.
LORD GORDON: Could you organize for the right to drink gin,
    Jack?
MR MANNERS: We've already had gin riots, Lord Gordon.
JACK: We want bread. Bread for everyone.
MARY: We have to ask for much more than bread.
JACK: The right to eat is important.
MARY: It's a right recognized only by the hungry. When the
    price of bread goes down everyone will go back to sleep.

53

No, we need something deeper, more imaginative, big
enough to net the future.

JACK: All men are born equal.

MR MANNERS: Too general, too general. We don't listen to
abstractions in England.

MARY: If we found a good phrase, a rallying cry, the rest would
focus naturally.

MR MANNERS: Yes. Think of the frenzy for Wilkes and
liberty . . .

LORD GORDON: What about Silks and tyranny? (*Pause*.) Milk
and bigotry?
(*Silence*.)
There's a Wilkes in the House. Tory chap, isn't he?

MR MANNERS: He's calmed down since the sixties. The House
does that.

JACK: Liberty. We'd go for that.

MARY: Yes. Liberty is a beautiful word.

MR MANNERS: Dangerous, Mary.

GUARD: Will there be liberty in the new world?

MARY: Oh yes. (*To* MR MANNERS) Why dangerous? It's what
we want.

MR MANNERS: Too hazy. No one will react to the word liberty.
It's been heard before and no one understands it.

MARY: Are you certain?

MR MANNERS: Why should I deceive you? People were shouting
for Wilkes not for liberty.

LORD GORDON: Gordon . . . What about Gordon and drollery?
I do so wish to hear my name shouted.

MARY: It seems to me that to build a new world one must first
tear down the old. We must know what people most want
to be rid of and from that clearing what we want will
emerge. What do you most dislike, Jack?

JACK: Hunger. I want to kill those who make us hungry.

MR MANNERS: That won't do.

MARY: Shouldn't we hear the people?

MR MANNERS: We want to lead them not to hear them.

MARY: Hear to lead.

LORD GORDON: You said I could be the leader in this, Mr

Manners. You said I could make myself known in history.

MR MANNERS: You will, Lord Gordon.

LORD GORDON: I know: the French!

MARY: What about the French?

LORD GORDON: What I most dislike. Hate them. Riot against 'em: No French.

MARY: That's called war and we already have one. It is our own country we want to purify. Sophie, what do you hate?

SOPHIE: Me? I don't know. Bad smells.

JACK: My sweet Sophie.

LORD GORDON: Told you it was the French. No French food. That'll rouse 'em.

MR MANNERS: (*To* MARY) There's a clue.

MARY: What makes a smell good or bad?

LORD GORDON: I don't know, but I know it when I smell it.

GUARD: What do smells have to do with the new world?

MRS TEMPTWELL: There won't be a new world.

JACK: I don't understand any of this. I'll organize for bread and liberty.

MRS TEMPTWELL: Go quickly before it's too late.

SOPHIE: No, Jack. Mary will help us. She's thinking for us.

MARY: I want us all to think together. A dog smells danger and barks at the intruder.

MR MANNERS: The foreigner.

MARY: Our lives ought by nature to be just, pleasant and free but we've been invaded by unnatural practices and beliefs. We must name them and bark. Who are the intruders?

MR MANNERS: In England it's the Dutch, but who could get emotional about them? The Jews . . . not enough of them. The Irish.

JACK: I hate the Irish, they work for lower wages and we can't find work.

LORD GORDON: Off with their heads.

MRS TEMPTWELL: They work, like you. Don't you see they're making you turn against your own kind?

MARY: Mrs Temptwell is right. We must not turn against working people.

MR MANNERS: The principle, however, is right. Ideas come

55

embodied in people. Get rid of the people, the rest follows.

MARY: What do all foreigners have in common?

LORD GORDON: They're not English.

MR MANNERS: Not Church of England.

JACK: We don't like the Church.

MARY: No. Anything that encourages superstition and prejudice is vile.

MR MANNERS: That's not the Church of England. After all, the Church of England is more England than Church. The superstitions remain from the Catholics. Yes. That's it. The Catholics.

MARY: The Catholics?

LORD GORDON: I'm to lead a mob of Catholics?

MR MANNERS: You can't lead any mob, Gordon, you're in Parliament. But you can present a petition. There's a bill in the house which will give back to Catholics their right to own property. There's already fear it will cause trouble. After all; there isn't that much property to go around.

MARY: What do you think of Catholics, Jack?

JACK: I don't know much. They do smoky things on Sundays.

MR MANNERS: It's much worse than that, isn't it, Mary?

MARY: Is it?

MR MANNERS: Now is the time for you to use your mind, Mary. Tell Jack about the Catholics. Tell him how they stuff themselves with white bread on Sundays.

MARY: Yes. They buy it all up and keep it in their chapels. That's why there's none for you.

MR MANNERS: The Pope has stores of bread in his palaces. He ships it secretly from England. He loves to eat Protestant bread.

MARY: He would prefer to eat Protestants, he makes them starve instead.

JACK: Where is this Pope? I'll kill him.

MARY: All Catholics are the Pope's slaves. If he told them to mix the blood of Protestant children with their wine, they would.

MR MANNERS: Protestant children have been known to disappear near Catholic chapels.

SOPHIE: Help!

MARY: It's the Catholics who've enclosed all the common land so they could build their chapels underground.

MRS TEMPTWELL: Oh!

MR MANNERS: Very good, Mary, that's right.

MARY: All over the world men groan in chains to build the Pope's palaces of luxury and depravity.

MR MANNERS: Actually the Pope is a woman. Her red robe is dyed anew every year in putrid blood.

LORD GORDON: I say, that's disgusting.

MARY: The Pope washes his hands in the blood of Protestant babes and his face in the tears of Protestant mothers.

SOPHIE: Help. No Catholics.

MR MANNERS: That's not quite right.

MARY: Popery is the eternal enslavement of the mind, the abject worship of a purple idol, the crawling of the dumb beast.

JACK: No to Popery, yes to Liberty.

MR MANNERS: Excellent. I think we should leave out the liberty for the moment.

LORD GORDON: No Popery. Is that what the petition says?

MR MANNERS: The petition is against the Catholic Repeal Act.

MARY: We'll explain that later, we must rouse the people. Stop English babies from being roasted. No Popery.

SOPHIE: Save the children. No Hopery.

MARY: No. It's no Popery.

JACK: Save the working people. No Popery.

GUARD: This new world . . .

MARY: Later, later. No slavery, no poverty, no Popery.

MRS TEMPTWELL: No fences. No Popery.

ALL: No Popery.

(*They knock over the chairs.* MARY *takes a torch. They chant.*)

ALL: NO POPERY.

The streets of London. MARY, MR MANNERS, LORD GORDON.

MR MANNERS: There are at least sixty thousand assembling in
  St George's Fields.

MARY: A headless snake winding its way towards Westminster
  Bridge. Thousands obeying our silent bidding. I'm
  breathless.

LORD GORDON: I'm a little nervous too.

MARY: It's time for you to go, Lord Gordon.

MR MANNERS: Do you have the petition ready?

LORD GORDON: Here, in my hand. Both hands.

MR MANNERS: Present it at two-thirty. Parliament is certain to
  delay consideration of a petition. Go out and announce this
  to the crowd.

MARY: Tell them you believe Parliament is on the side of the
  Catholics.

LORD GORDON: There are so many of them. I won't be hurt,
  will I?

MARY: Hurry, Lord Gordon. They're moving fast now.

LORD GORDON: I never liked crowds.

MARY: If you don't go, they'll surround Parliament and you
  won't be able to get in.

LORD GORDON: It's not an easy thing to become a historical
  figure.
  (*He goes.*)

MARY: Thousands and I've roused them. Oh, this is a delight
  beyond anything. Aren't you enjoying yourself?

MR MANNERS: No. I like quiet. I'll be happy when it's over.

MARY: But this is a beginning. A new surge which I shall lead.

MR MANNERS: To what?

MARY: To happiness. No more impotent anger. Let
  imaginations be free and construct their own world.

MR MANNERS: You could be very useful, Mary, but you have a
  lot to learn. Power, however, is a brilliant master.

MARY: No, no more rulers. I want to teach them to be their

own rulers.

MR MANNERS: That won't last long.

MARY: I'll guide them, of course.

MR MANNERS: So. You are learning. Ah, listen. Shouts. The crowd's beginning to be unruly. It usually takes an hour or two, a few well-placed rumours.

(SOPHIE *and* JACK *come on.*)

SOPHIE: Parliament won't save us from the Catholics.

JACK: We'll save ourselves from the Catholics.

SOPHIE: We went to Duke Street.

JACK: Where there are many Catholics.

SOPHIE: We found the chapel of the ambassador from Gardenia.

MARY: Gardenia?

SOPHIE: It's a Popist island, they capture Protestant ships and make shoes from the bones of sailors. They speak horrible spells in ill-latin.

MARY: Sardinia.

JACK: No Popery and wooden shoes. We burnt the chapel.

SOPHIE: No Popery.

JACK: We're looking for the Bavarian chapel.

SOPHIE: Burn it. No Popery.

(*They go off.*)

MARY: Let's go. Let's go and lead them all.

MR MANNERS: Power always moves from behind. Let the bodies move forward.

MARY: I'm drunk with what I've done. All those people swaying at my thoughts: glory.

(*The* GUARD *comes on.*)

GUARD: We're thousands but act like one. We have the strength to build the new world. Yes, we'll have all we want, we'll share it, we're one.

MARY: Yes. Yes. And it's by my command. I've done it all.

(JACK *and* SOPHIE *come on.*)

JACK: The Bavarian embassy: burnt. On to Wapping. Find the Catholic houses and throw all contents on to the street. Burn, burn it all. There's a house belongs to a Protestant manufacturer, we're going to leave it, but someone shouts: why? Catholic or not, why should anyone be possessed of

59

more than a thousand a year? Yes. Why? Burn it to the ground.

SOPHIE: No Popery. Freedom for all. Set the Protestant prisoners free. To Newgate. To Bridewell. No Popery. To Clerkenwell.

(*They rush off.*)

MARY: This burning makes me a little uneasy, Mr Manners.

MR MANNERS: If you want to chop wood, you must expect the chips to fly. Are you afraid?

MARY: No indeed.

MR MANNERS: It has never been possible to define freedom.

MARY: What?

MR MANNERS: Nothing. It's getting dark. Shapes lose their firmness.

(JACK *comes on, followed by* SOPHIE.)

SOPHIE: Lord Gordon has presented the petition five times and Parliament has refused to consider it five times. And now they want to go home and sleep. We're rough handling the ones we catch. Let them dare come out.

JACK: We're collecting for the poor mob. Give to the poor mob. For the poor mob.

SOPHIE: Here. Here's a penny for the poor mob. But I am the poor mob.

(*The* GUARD *comes on.*)

GUARD: No Popery and wooden shoes. To Holborn.

JACK: To Holborn.

SOPHIE: Holborn.

(*They go.*)

MARY: Why Holborn?

MR MANNERS: Streets of distilleries. And they all belong to Catholics, or so the rumour goes.

MARY: I don't understand. I feel so powerful I can't think any more. Look. Fire.

MR MANNERS: There are twenty thousand gallons of gin in those houses.

MARY: Oh God!

MR MANNERS: God?

(MRS TEMPTWELL *comes on, slowly. She speaks coldly and*

quietly to MARY.)

MRS TEMPTWELL: It was dark, only a few thousand of us left. Prisoners, enthusiasts, those who couldn't free themselves from the throe of the crowd. We heard, to Holborn. We moved, step by step, pushed, pushing. Torches were at the front. We spread along the street. We heard there was gin inside the houses, gin to refresh the poor people. We rushed in, we fell in, against the houses, torches high. I was pushed, I dropped, on my knees, drank the liquid, warm, then burning, looked up to see all coated in flames, fire rippling along the gin, houses, people, clothes, all burning. (*Pause.*)
Bodies pushed each other into the burning river, slid, still trying to drink, lapped at the fire. Women, children, tearing their clothes off, people laughed. Laughed. A man next to me tore off his clothes, found a girl, rolled her into the fire, pulled off her skirts. A wall crumbled over them.

MARY: Stop.

MRS TEMPTWELL: Arms, arms waved underneath bodies, hundreds of arms, shouting, waving, dogs snapping at the edge of hell. A woman grabbed me. 'I was just looking,' she said, 'why me?' Her cindered scalp peeled off.

MARY: Stop it!

MRS TEMPTWELL: The smell, it was the smell. I fainted, slept. All quiet, the fire on to other houses. Moved a leg, shoved a body off me, crawled on a soft cushion of corpses, black, nothing much left.

MARY: It's not true. It didn't happen.

MRS TEMPTWELL: Yes? Your precious world? You don't believe me?
(MRS TEMPTWELL *opens a bundle she's been carrying, ashes and bones, and throws them over* MARY.)

MRS TEMPTWELL: Look carefully through the teeth and you'll find some gold.

MARY: No! No! It cannot have happened.
(JACK *runs on, his clothes smouldering.*)

JACK: Water. I'm burning. Gin. The working man's in flames. Help. Help me.

(SOPHIE *rushes to him.*)

SOPHIE: Jack! Jack! (*She laughs, drunk*) We've burnt
everything. No Popery. No nothing. Jack. Damn them.
Damn everything, Jack.
(*She punches him, laughing. They fall over and roll together.*)

MARY: Oh, my sweet Sophie, no.
(*The* GUARD *comes on.*)

GUARD: Where's my new world, where is it? Where?
(GILES TRAVERSE *comes on.*)

GILES: They're moving towards the Bank of England, Mr
Manners.

MR MANNERS: Ah. That must be stopped.

GILES: (*To* MARY) So, you've been involved in this horror?

MARY: It wasn't meant to be like this, please believe me. I had
dreams.

GILES: I know. Your own voices.

MARY: I listened to others.

GILES: And they turned to nightmares.

MARY: Help me.

GILES: How can I? You're accountable now.

MR MANNERS: Tell them to send the soldiers, Giles.

GILES: It's about time.

MR MANNERS: And for the soldiers to shoot.

MARY: No.

GILES: You can't do that, Mr Manners.

MR MANNERS: I believe I know best.

GILES: You can't let the mob rampage for three days and shoot
them now.

MR MANNERS: If you do not agree with our policies, Giles, you
need not stay with us.

GILES: This isn't policy, this is crime.

MARY: This isn't what I wanted!

GILES: Will we ever know what we want?
(*He leaves.*)

MARY: Don't let them shoot. Don't.

MR MANNERS: There is nothing so cleansing as massive death.
People return with such relief to their private little
sufferings and stop barking at the future. Believe me, it's

what they want. This will last forty years at least, forty years of rule and order.

MARY: Damn your order and your rules.

MR MANNERS: Don't damn the rules, Mary. Rules keep you from feeling pain and emptiness. They bring peace to the heart, they're clear and simple, they hide the lengthening shadows. I'll do anything to keep the rules safe, not only for myself, for the happiness of the world. One day all men will understand how beautiful they are, and worship as I do.

(LORD GORDON *rushes on.*)

LORD GORDON: They say it's my fault, they want to arrest me, save me, Mr Manners.

MR MANNERS: We will, give us time. Go to them now.

LORD GORDON: (*To* MARY) I've just remembered where I saw you. I didn't mean to, that is, I didn't know who you – that is, it didn't seem to matter, but it – they're coming for me. It was better to be nobody.

(*He runs off. The shooting is heard.*)

MARY: Please, please tell me it isn't so.

(*She screams. The shooting continues.*)

MRS TEMPTWELL: (*Who has been piling the bones into a neat little pile*) One. Ten, fifteen, one hundred, five hundred, one thousand, ten thousand, three million, six million, thirty eight, two hundred, five, three, one.

MARY: Please tell me it did not happen.

ACT FOUR

SCENE ONE

Lodgings near Tyburn. SOPHIE *has a baby in her arms.* MRS
TEMPTWELL *tries to get near her.*

SOPHIE: I love her.

MRS TEMPTWELL: That's a title to nothing. Give her to me.

SOPHIE: I've looked after her well.

MRS TEMPTWELL: You always were a fool.

SOPHIE: I want to see Miss Mary.

MRS TEMPTWELL: Do as you're told.

> (MARY *comes on. She's half-dressed, a mess. She drags herself
> to a chair and collapses.*)

MARY: Find a shoe for my right foot, Mrs Temptwell.

MRS TEMPTWELL: I don't know where they are.

> (MARY *kicks off her one shoe.*)

MARY: There. Order. No. It seems I need a stocking.

> (*She stares vacantly at one of her legs, then rolls down her one
> stocking. She stops.*)

> Leave it. Nature's a mess. What are you doing here,
> Sophie?

SOPHIE: You wanted to see your child.

MARY: Did I?

MRS TEMPTWELL: The future citizen of the new world.

MARY: Stop. Yes, I know. The child. The last act.

SOPHIE: Let me take her back to the country with me. We're
very happy. Jack is coming soon.

MARY: Jack.

MRS TEMPTWELL: Remember the working man?

SOPHIE: They'll let him go soon, he didn't do anything.

MRS TEMPTWELL: You don't have to do anything to get
yourself killed. Give us the child.

SOPHIE: Why? Why can't I stay?

MARY: Don't use that fateful word, Sophie. Has that woman
tempted you as well? Run.

MRS TEMPTWELL: You did it yourself, you did it to us.

MARY: Did I? I wanted knowledge, Sophie, but I didn't know

64

what it was. I felt a lover's desire for the world and if I sought to undress it, it was only for a closer embrace. No one told me I'd hug stinking bones, caress putrefaction. Even God wouldn't love this world, if he existed, and I know he doesn't because Voltaire said so and Voltaire is a wit, and the truth can only be funny. You never laugh, Sophie.

SOPHIE: What will you do with her?

MARY: You see the two of us here, crumbling slowly. It won't be long now. Our hearts are charred. We're too crippled by what we've seen to scavenge for more hope. Soon we can stop breathing – last intake of the future. But it's not enough. Our death won't redeem what's been. New flesh, new bones will pursue new illusion, new crimes. I find that unacceptable. I am human, I know the world, I've shared its acts. And I would like to pour poison down the throat of this world, burn out its rotting guts, obliterate its hideous memories. Cancel the past, cancel it all, from the beginning, murder, misery, starvation, torture, torment. How? I don't know. But I can start here. I can look after what I've generated. Stop it. That's the immediate. We'll see about the rest.

SOPHIE: You want to poison your daughter.

MRS TEMPTWELL: We're all poisoned anyway.

MARY: Spare the future the danger of her dreams. Spare her the ashen taste of exhausted ideas. Listen to me. There is no reason to be in the world, and no reason for the world to be. It follows the world must not be. The end. Don't make me say any more. I'm tired. Be reasonable. Be human. Allow us to kill in peace.

SOPHIE: No. You can't do that.

MARY: Is there anything we are not capable of?

SOPHIE: Listen to me. You don't know.

MRS TEMPTWELL: She knows everything. She just told you.

SOPHIE: You're wrong. There is. I know. I know about things you don't.

MRS TEMPTWELL: Our Sophie's finding her tongue.

MARY: Just when I want silence.

SOPHIE: Listen to me.

MRS TEMPTWELL: Must be the country air. Pink cheeks, pink thoughts.

SOPHIE: Stop. Don't you dare. I will make you listen.

MARY: Surely you must hate the world as much as I do?

SOPHIE: I don't. I don't at all. I know. I know – about mornings.

MARY: The mornings?

MRS TEMPTWELL: Milking the landlord's cows, haha.

SOPHIE: The first light of the morning. Fresh, new. I feel a kind of hunger, but without the pain. The grass is wet and soft. Cold water on the skin. It makes her laugh too. Think about the mornings, how they're free.

MRS TEMPTWELL: Corpses look very fresh in the morning. You can go.

SOPHIE: No I won't. Not until I've explained. The sound of the wind, how it changes. Drops of water on the roof when you're inside and warm. An old woman touches your face, wishes you well. Don't you understand?

MARY: I don't think I want to.

MRS TEMPTWELL: We don't need an upstart bumpkin preaching to us. Go.

SOPHIE: I will not. Miss Mary is unhappy about the world, but you, Mrs Temptwell, are full of hate. She hates you, Mary, she always did.

MARY: Did she? Yes, I knew. I forgot to ask why.

SOPHIE: Your father took her land.

MARY: I remember. My uncle killed her grandmother.

SOPHIE: She wants to kill your child to punish you. She only wants to hurt you.

MARY: Is that true, Mrs Temptwell?
(*Pause.*)
I suppose it's fair.

SOPHIE: No. It's not the way. It's wrong.

MARY: Not wrong, Sophie, but small. As small as everything else. I thought we shared a noble despair, but that was another illusion. It's a habit. The world is made up of small particles of unspeakable ugliness, why expect common

66

understanding? The devil at least would have had an intellect. You had to be a woman, base, selfish. Well. Why should I have the arrogance to claim unique pain? Why didn't you just strangle me in my cradle?

MRS TEMPTWELL: I was as innocent as you. I thought it was enough to humiliate you, make you as dirty as me.

MARY: And now?

MRS TEMPTWELL: I understand about you now, your kind. I hate you, Mary, I hate your father, I hate your child, not any more for what you did to me, but for what you are. You're the evil spirits, your kind, you cast the spells that keep us bound, to die for you. Everything you touch goes wrong, but you save yourselves and then go all poetic over other people's bodies. I know all we need is your death, the death of all of you, and then it won't go wrong again, then there will be a new world.

MARY: More burning, more bones.

MRS TEMPTWELL: The right bones. I'll laugh when I touch the ashes of thy kind, Mary Traverse.

MARY: I see. (*Pause*.) Perhaps you're right. I've been greedy, I'm bloated, I must go. But I believe you may simply be addicted to counting bodies. And greed can attach itself to anyone. It doesn't matter. I'll kill the child if I don't feel too tired. If not, you can. Despair is an opiate that numbs itself. I want to sleep.

SOPHIE: Wait. You don't know how to think, Mary. You think at a distance, you're always ahead, or too far back. If you looked – just looked from near, I know it would be different. Look out of the window. Just look.

MRS TEMPTWELL: We took these lodgings to watch men on their way to be hanged at Tyburn. It's very restful.

SOPHIE: If you look, at a smoothly built wall, at a hedge of beeches, you'll see you can't decide for anyone else. I know you can't.

MARY: The child is mine, I can decide her future.

SOPHIE: She's not yours, let her decide, she's free.

MARY: I'm tired. Give her to me before I fall asleep.

MRS TEMPTWELL: The crowds are coming. It's the best

67

attended amusement in London.

(SOPHIE *takes the child a little away and sings a beautiful song.*)

MARY: Listen.

MRS TEMPTWELL: Shouts for the hanging.

MARY: Listen to Sophie. How beautifully she sings. I hope death will be as sweet. Ha, a gracenote there. An old song, conceived in hope, embellished by an artist, soothes a child, would rock to sleep the pangs of conscience. Do I have it all wrong? What are you looking at, Sophie, what do you see?

MRS TEMPTWELL: Crowds drooling.

MARY: Soft grey lines sloping against the London sky.

SOPHIE: Look at the stone. The carved stone.

MARY: Yes, I see. The new houses. With what care they've worked the stone. Those are hands that loved the matter of the world, they knew about your mornings. Do I have it all wrong?

SOPHIE: I can show you many things done by good hands. There are other ways than to poison and scream.

MARY: Sing, Sophie. If I were God your song would appease me and I would forgive the world.

SOPHIE: Touch your baby's skin. It's the same thing.

MRS TEMPTWELL: There's the cart. See who's in there, Sophie, and then sing to us.

SCENE TWO

Tyburn. SOPHIE, MRS TEMPTWELL, *and* MARY, *holding her baby. A* MAN *pulls a cart.* JACK *is inside, alone.* LORD EXRAKE *follows.*

SOPHIE: (*Screams*) Jack! Jack!

MARY: I thought it would be Lord Gordon.

MRS TEMPTWELL: You don't like to hang lords.

MARY: How can I convince you I am not them.

SOPHIE: Jack. Speak to me. Jack.

(JACK *is silent.*)

MAN: Let the cart pass.

68

LORD EXRAKE: Is he going to say something?

MARY: Lord Exrake.

LORD EXRAKE: Hello, my dear. Who are you? Forgive me . . . My memory . . . what a sweet child. Not mine, I hope. No: too young. These days . . .

SOPHIE: Jack. It's me. Sophie. Speak to me.

(JACK *is silent*.)

LORD EXRAKE: Sophie . . . Means wisdom. I have loved . . . Did you ask why I'm here? I've found a way to go to sleep. I listen to what they say before they're hanged. I repeat their last words and it makes me sleep. Try it.

MARY: Is there no grace, somewhere?

LORD EXRAKE: (*To the* MAN) When will he talk?

MAN: Don't know. Some of them make jokes at the end. Some tell their lives, give speeches. I've never seen one who wouldn't talk.

LORD EXRAKE: Silence. Silence at the very end. Would that make me sleep?

SOPHIE: (*To* MARY) You know he didn't do anything. Tell them.

MARY: Who will listen?

MRS TEMPTWELL: Sing to her, Sophie.

MAN: (*To* JACK) Look, I know how you feel. Animals out there, aren't they? But you have a wife, right? Someone, anyway. Children? Well, there's a way you can take care of them when you're dead. Nothing magic. I work for this man: all you have to do is say this word we tell you and we'll look after your widow and any woman. What about it?

SOPHIE: Jack!

MAN: Look, she's crying for you. You don't want her to go hungry, do you? All you have to say, before the man – you know. Just before. All you say is: Drink Olvitie. Got it? Drink Olvitie. That's all.

LORD EXRAKE: That's what a man said a few weeks ago. Drink Olvitie. I've been drinking it ever since.

MAN: Remember that: drink Olvitie and she'll be looked after.

SOPHIE: (*To* MARY) You did all this. You should be up there. Go on. Kill your child. Here, I'll put it under the wheel for you.

MARY: Oh Sophie, not now. Not from you. Remember what you've said. I know we can find . . . we will.

MRS TEMPTWELL: You won't.

LORD EXRAKE: Have you lost something, my dear? Perhaps I can help you. What won't she find?

MRS TEMPTWELL: Grace. She hasn't the right.

SOPHIE: Jack!

MARY: We will grieve, Sophie, but we won't despair. Come with me.

(MARY *takes* SOPHIE *in her arms. She turns away her head.* JACK *stares impassive. Silence.*)

LORD EXRAKE: Silence. Not even a curse.

SCENE THREE

A garden in the Potteries. MARY, SOPHIE, GILES, *little* MARY.

GILES: What are you looking at, Mary?

MARY: The light on the river, Father. It's so beautiful. I want to touch it. But we can't even see light. Perhaps one day we'll understand it.

GILES: You mustn't try to understand everything.

MARY: Why not?

SOPHIE: When you told me the world was made up of little particles, Mary, I cried for days. I was afraid to walk on the grass, it felt dark.

MARY: But eventually beauty seeps back through the darkness. Nature is vain and preens itself.

GILES: I was unhappy when I found out how old the world was. It seemed so mortal.

MARY: And yet, I love your wrinkles, I read a life in them, it is interesting.

GILES: There are still some things it is better not to know, others it is best to forget. Sophie agrees with me.

SOPHIE: No. I don't think we should forget.

(*Short pause.*)

MARY: And now the light lifts itself off the river. A streak on the chimneys. Gone. The world's been sparkling all the time and we've been too distracted to look.

GILES: It's getting chilly. Shall I take little Mary in?

(MRS TEMPTWELL *comes on. A pause.*)

MRS TEMPTWELL: I have come to my father's land.

GILES: Yes.

MRS TEMPTWELL: Try to throw me off.

GILES: No. Those days are past. That much I have learned.

MRS TEMPTWELL: What can you have learned?

GILES: Oh, many things. Not to take orders. Not to give them.
Not to want to give them. But I'm old. Speak to them.

(MARY *and* SOPHIE *are standing side by side.*)

SOPHIE: I thought it was enough to look, but it isn't. There
needs to be much more. I see that now.

MARY: Beauty –

SOPHIE: Not just seen by day. Another beauty underlies it,
doesn't disappear at night. Find that too.

MARY: And when we know this beauty, Sophie, not just
nature's, but the beauty recreated by those who have lived
in the world, will we learn – not to forget, no – but at least
to forgive history?

SOPHIE: I don't know. We can try.

MARY: I'm certain that when we understand it all, it'll be
simpler, not more confusing. One day we'll know how to
love this world.

SOPHIE: We'll see.

MARY: It's all we have.

SOPHIE: Yes. It's all we have.

(*Fade.*)